PRAISE FOR *CARNE DE DIOS*

"The Beat poets stoned in Mexico were all María Sabina's visionary children."

—LAWRENCE FERLINGHETTI
co-founder of City Lights Booksellers

"Maria Sabina—great seer and poet of Indigenous Mexico and the world—sets the ground in this powerful fantasy of worlds in alignment and collision. Sabina's ritual litanies meet Beat seekers of trance and travel, and one thinks of the ecstatic litanies of Ginsberg's 'Howl.' The transcendent poetry and vocal elements in Homero Aridjis's rich book of consociational poetic Time and sacred Space keep the universe aspin. What a great conjoining."

—ANNE WALDMAN,
author of *Fast Speaking Woman*

"Imagine a batch of Holy Children (i.e., magic mushrooms) colliding with a batch of unholy Beatniks in a remote part of Mexico. Such a collision resulted in this simultaneously surreal, lyrical, comic, and brutal Mexican novel expertly translated by Chloe Garcia Roberts."

—LAWRENCE MILLMAN
author of *Fungipedia*

"It is with a poet's touch, honed over many years of practice, that Homero Aridjis reimagines a world in which figures from the Beat past coincide with the shadow presence of the real and legendary Mazatec shaman/poet María Sabina. By turns a fiction and a work of poesis, Aridjis's book chronicles a juncture and a clash of actors and symbols that is the mark of the greatest poetry of our time and of all others."

—JEROME ROTHENBERG,
author of *Technicians of the Sacred*

"One of Latin America's finest pens, the book we've all been waiting for! Aridjis renders a true-to-life portrait of the mysterious curandera whose name has become synonymous with the medicine of 'magic' mushrooms and 1960s hippie counterculture. A woman, small in stature but immense in reputation, from the mountains of Oaxaca, who has captured the global and cultural imagination for more than half a century, María Sabina, is depicted here with the grace and reverence her legacy deserves, while at the same time raising questions about the appropriation that has long been a pastime of norteamericanos seeking an ethnic—and dare I say, magical—experience south of the border. Only a novelist, poet, and environmentalist of Aridjis's skill and position could handle such a delicate subject and make it a compelling read. And this careful translation offered by Chloe Garcia Roberts wholly elevates the textual and visual experience of Aridjis's writing. What an achievement! What a story!"

—TIM Z. HERNANDEZ
author of *They Call You Back*

"*Carne de Dios* re-creates the world of Mazatec poet and shaman María Sabina (1894–1985), whose mushroom ceremonies brought the U.S. Beat generation to Mexico in search of esoteric knowledge, drugs, and sex. Homero Aridjis, Mexico's greatest living poet, overturns much of the mythology surrounding Beat mysticism as it comes face-to-face with an ancient spiritual tradition. This artful and accomplished translation brings Aridjis's vision to life and captures the extraordinary power and insight of his poetics so well that the reader may wonder if they, too, are hallucinating as they read."

—JAMES LÓPEZ
University of Tampa

CARNE DE DIOS

CAMINO DEL SOL

A LATINX LITERARY SERIES

RIGOBERTO GONZÁLEZ, SERIES EDITOR

HOMERO ARIDJIS

TRANSLATED BY CHLOE GARCIA ROBERTS

CARNE DE DIOS

A NOVEL

THE UNIVERSITY OF
ARIZONA PRESS
TUCSON

The University of Arizona Press
www.uapress.arizona.edu

We respectfully acknowledge the University of Arizona is on the land and territories of Indigenous peoples. Today, Arizona is home to twenty-two federally recognized tribes, with Tucson being home to the O'odham and the Yaqui. Committed to diversity and inclusion, the University strives to build sustainable relationships with sovereign Native Nations and Indigenous communities through education offerings, partnerships, and community service.

ISBN-13: 978-0-8165-5414-0 (paperback)
ISBN-13: 978-0-8165-5415-7 (ebook)

Cover design by Leigh McDonald
Cover art by Santiago Moyao
Designed and typeset by Leigh McDonald in Adobe Jenson Pro 10.5/14, Romana, and Lato (display)

Originally published as *Carne de Dios* by Alfaguara, 2015.

Publication of this book is made possible in part by the proceeds of a permanent endowment created with the assistance of a Challenge Grant from the National Endowment for the Humanities, a federal agency.

Chloe Garcia Roberts wishes to acknowledge the NEA for awarding her a 2021 fellowship in translation, which aided in the completion of this work.

Library of Congress Cataloging-in-Publication Data are available on the final page of this volume.

Printed in the United States of America
♾ This paper meets the requirements of ANSI/NISO Z39.48-1992 (Permanence of Paper).

CONTENTS

INTRODUCTION

Carne de Dios, "God meat" in Spanish, is a translation of Teonanácatl, the Nahuatl name for a species of psilocybin-containing mushrooms native to the Mexican mountains. Homero Aridjis's novel *Carne de Dios* is the story of how these mushrooms came to spark the subsequent consciousness revolution of the 1960s, unleashing a wave of global interest in mushroom culture that is enjoying widespread resurgence today. It is the story of how and where it all began, high in the Sierra Madre de Oaxaca range, in a tiny mud-walled shack overlooking the remote town of Huautla de Jiménez, where a Mazatec single mother named María Sabina lived with her family and practiced as a healer using the sacred mushrooms.

Sabina lacked a formal education, did not know her own age, and never learned to speak Spanish. She discovered her ability to heal with the sacred mushrooms as a child and performed mushroom ceremonies, or *veladas,* throughout her life until achieving international fame in her sixties, when she attracted the attention of the burgeoning youth movement in the United States and Europe. Rock stars, writers, businessmen, scientists, politicians, poets, beatniks, and seekers of all kinds flocked to the tiny town of Huautla de Jiménez to meet María Sabina and try to attend one of her ceremonies. Her veladas were recorded, filmed, transcribed, studied, and imitated. Samples of her mushrooms were taken to labs for analysis, experimentation, patenting, and production. She was surveilled, arrested, harassed by the local and federal levels of the Mexican government, and blamed for the tide of disruptive and drug-using foreigners flooding the area.

In his novel about this moment in time, 1957, when María Sabina and her abilities were the sudden subjects of global focus, Aridjis centers her as the vital source of the subsequent global interest in mushrooms and their medical and psychological potential. He begins *Carne de Dios* by describing the famed Mazatec mushroom priestess as being "no stranger to thresholds." It was this ability to cross these thresholds, to open communication between worlds, human and nonhuman, and to commune with the sacred mushrooms that immediately put her in the international spotlight after the American banker and amateur ethnomycologist R. Gordon Wasson's famous journey to experience the mushrooms was immortalized in *LIFE Magazine*. By detailing María Sabina's role in shaping world culture, Aridjis honors her as one of the greatest healers, poets, visionaries, and translators that Mexico has ever produced. As she stated in her own dictated autobiography, *Vida de María Sabina, la sabia de los hongos*, "[the sacred mushrooms] speak and I have the power to translate."

Carne de Dios is not just the story of María Sabina, however: it is also a story of the people who flocked to see her. It is not just the story of her life, but a story of the ways in which that life reverberated and collided with the lives of others and of how those concurrences still resonate today. It is also a story of cultural devastation. The novel is written in a series of interlinked vignettes, each of which conveys a slightly different atmosphere, depending on the character depicted. The sections span the absurd, the tragic, and the horrific. From the séance-like veladas to Sabina's stories from her own life to the varied and intertwined adventures of her devotees, the book is a narrative of and an arabesque on the central story of encounter, between the Mexica and other native populations and the invading Spanish, that is the backbone of Mexican identity, with each character illustrating, through their trajectories, the sweeping and irreversible change that inevitably happens as a result of all such meetings.

Up until Gordon Wasson's visit to Huautla, the use of ceremonial mushrooms was limited to the communities in which the traditions existed. His visit was a cultural encounter that marked the beginning of a larger modern understanding of the mushrooms and the gifts they contained. In his novel, however, Aridjis shows how these gifts cannot be disentangled from the personage of María Sabina; he also shows us how the global amplification of her talents was exploitative. Through a wide cast of characters that includes some of the most famous artists of the period as well as prominent scientists and Latin American cultural figures, Aridjis paints a portrait of these *extranjeros* searching out María Sabina with solely personal agendas, hoping to use her skills to achieve their own ends or address a particular lack in their lives. The portrait he paints of these seekers is damning.

Aridjis also focuses on the contrast of the two drug cultures by juxtaposing the sacred tradition of Sabina's mushroom veladas, conducted for healing those in need, with the foreigners' fixation on escape, obliteration, and fun. Nowhere are these differences more apparent than in the figure of the American patron saint of heroin addiction, William Burroughs, who wanders through this book like a murderous wraith, completely consumed and driven by his own violent and malicious appetites. He stands as an embodiment of the inhumanity of one type of drug culture in contrast to the humanity of María Sabina and her mushrooms.

The novel ends with the arrest of María Sabina and the expulsion of many of these extranjeros from Mexico. However, the book continues with an afterword by the author detailing his own personal encounter with Sabina toward the end of her life. Despite being a person of international influence and a direct link to money-making pharmaceutical developments and patents, María Sabina's poverty remained acute right up until her death in 1985. After discovering her dire health prognosis, Aridjis and his wife, the translator and editor Betty Ferber, arranged for her to come to Mexico City to live with them while receiving medical treatment. This personal encounter with Sabina shapes the book in various ways, but primarily it gives a gravity to the story, an awareness that she was in the end not compensated for the bestowal of her gifts. In her own words: "From the moment the foreigners arrived to search for God, the saint children [*niños santos*, her name for the mushrooms] lost their purity. They lost their force; they spoiled them. From now on they won't be of any use. There's no remedy for it. Before Wasson, I felt that the saint children elevated me. I don't feel like that anymore. The force has diminished."

Homero Aridjis is largely known as a poet in the United States, but he is also a prolific novelist whose muse is always Mexico. His novels are an antidote to a reductive view of its culture, geography, and history. To read one of his novels is to be schooled in both the broader forces and the minutiae that shape the place. Mexico in Aridjis's fiction is prismatic and ample, a sprawling, shifting, chaotic melee of characters, cultures, and ecosystems. His casts of characters are large and function as an ensemble, and each one represents a multitude of intentions, actions, and desires that defy simplification.

Aridjis is the author of over fifty novels and books of poetry. He has served as Mexico's ambassador to the Netherlands, Switzerland, and UNESCO, as well as the president of PEN International. He is an active outspoken advocate for Mexico's natural world—in particular as a protector of the monarch butterfly and its migration grounds—and is the founder and president of the Group of 100, an association of artists and scientists who advocate for environmental causes. He is also the last living character in Roberto Bolaño's *The Savage Detectives* and a revered figure in Mexican literature. All of these different arenas of experience come into play in his novels with a great depth of reference and detail.

Carne de Dios is a poet's novel, and my primary aim as translator was to maintain this character—that is, to focus on its structure as a novel told in vignettes, with each chapter being a complete aesthetic movement. I wanted to highlight the way Aridjis can paint a scene and leave it shining in the air for a moment—a man with bottle caps sewn on his shirt like military insignia silhouetted against a bougainvillea-covered wall, a soliloquy delivered by Jack Kerouac as he leans over a highway bridge looking for the lost prostitute Tristessa in a river of cars flashing by below him, a trapped eagle emerging from a box clutching a snake in a reenactment of the Mexica origin myth.

On a granular level, many of the original anthropological and scientific transcriptions of María Sabina's words have become a gospel of vocabulary surrounding her history. *Velada*, for example, which can be translated as "ceremony," I have left as *velada* at the request of the author, as he expressed the belief that no other word would do to describe these ceremonies. Some of the names of the sacred mushrooms have changed in this translation, however. *Niños santos*, for example, appear as "Holy Children" rather than "saint children." And, finally, the translations of Sabina's poems are my own, even though they are translations of translations. The originals were recorded in Mazatec and then later translated into Spanish; the latter served as my source.

Homero knew Sabina, as he details in his afterword. He's told me that their conversations when she was staying with his family are woven throughout the book, so even in this work of fiction there are moments of truth in her words. The effect is of a layering of time, as her words from the end of her life come out of her mouth decades earlier. The novel is also populated by real people, many of whom are artists. Kerouac, Allen Ginsberg, and Juan Rulfo are just some of the literary figures who appear here, and their writings blend with those of their fictional contemporaries in a unique way. Like in a dream, a figure can at any point in the novel walk out of the reality of history and into a conversation with the fictional. Memories, works of art, and historical happenings collide in these pages, and it is sometimes hard to tell where one state ends and another begins. This blurring creates a particular atmosphere that I wanted to render in English, a haziness, a hallucinogenic quality, a feel of its being a novel under the influence.

While I have taken on many other translation projects in Spanish, my father tongue, this is the first that is from Mexico. Mexico is a country that I am both a part of and apart from, and it has been an honor to translate a novel about one of its most vital voices written by one of its most revered literary ones. My hope is that both figures gain wider recognition for their contributions and that this translation might in some small way assist in that.

As I worked with Homero on this novel over the years, on each trip home to see my father and family, I would also visit his and Betty's house in Mexico City. Over long lunches in their magical home filled with works of art, books, and jars overflowing with monarch butterfly wings, we would discuss notes and questions about the novel, but also politics, art, and Mexican history. Then, when I was back at home in the States, Aridjis's words would take me on other journeys, as I researched everything from mountain ranges and geological formations around Oaxaca to local political organizations, from the history of slavery in the country to the design of cigarette boxes in the 1950s. I watched medicinal commercials from the time, learned about traditional Mazatec dances, and discovered Mexican nicknames for mambo stars. Mostly done during the COVID-19 pandemic, this work was a daily affirmation that the world is larger and richer than the immediate; it was an opportunity to take a trip when I needed it most. If the Mexico of an Aridjis novel is a teeming, roiling tapestry, then in the task of rendering his work into English, I have been surprised to find my own minute thread adding to its weave.

This sense of circling and returning extends even to the figure of María Sabina herself. One Christmas a long time ago my family drove from Mexico City to Oaxaca at night under a full moon. After we were out of the city and over the mountains, the plains enveloped us. Everything was light and darkness—there were no halftones—and as the car sped along, its shadow, projected on the desert hills on either side of the highway, sliced the moonlight into bands of strobing black and white. Somehow, when I think back to that night, it has become fused with a black-and-white image that my brother bought on that trip—the jagged face of a smoking Sabina that later hung on the wall of our New York City apartment for years when we were growing up. Now the memory has morphed, and in my mind our small car is driving across her face, a face that was a witness of my childhood and toward which I feel some great, mysterious, and profound debt.

Chloe Garcia Roberts
August 2024

CARNE DE DIOS

teunanacatlth, que quiere decir carne de dios

FRAY TORIBIO DE BENAVENTE, MEMORIALES

If the doors of perception were cleansed, everything would appear to man as it is, infinite.

WILLIAM BLAKE, *PROVERBS OF HELL*

There I was, poised in space, a disembodied eye, invisible, incorporeal, seeing but not seen.

R. GORDON WASSON, "SEEKING THE MAGIC MUSHROOM"

Des mots, des couleurs, des peurs, des incertitudes sortis de quelque rêve mexicain.

HENRI MICHAUX, IN HIS DEDICATION TO BETTY AND HOMERO ARIDJIS IN THEIR COPY OF *MISÉRABLE MIRACLE*

I saw the best minds of my generation destroyed by madness.

ALLEN GINSBERG, "HOWL"

En cierto tiempo vinieron jóvenes de uno y otro sexo, de largas cabelleras, con vestiduras extrañas. Vestían camisas de variados colores y usaban collares. Vinieron muchos. Algunos me buscaban para que yo me desvelara con el pequeño que brota. "Venimos a buscar a Dios," decían.

MARÍA SABINA, *VIDA DE MARÍA SABINA, LA SABIA DE LOS HONGOS*

1

SHAMAN OF HALLUCINATIONS

María Sabina was no stranger to thresholds. She saw invisible beings. The sacred mushrooms spoke through her, using her voice.

Thin, short, and barefoot, this Señora Without Stain didn't remember her own age, but she remembered the years of visions and of death. She didn't know how to read, or how to write, or how to speak Spanish. Born in Huautla de Jiménez, she lived her entire life in this town among the hills, working the land to feed herself and her children.

Her dress was simple: an ankle-length petticoat and a huipil of white muslin decorated with colored ribbons and embroidered with yellow birds and pink flowers. When she left the house, she wrapped herself in a rebozo, handwoven on a backstrap loom, wide enough to hold a nursing infant or to carry mushrooms gathered under a new moon.

On Sundays, between nine and eleven in the morning, she went down to the market to sell corn, beans, and coffee. These were the most bustling hours in Huautla, whose people, according to the myths of their ancestors, the first Mazatec speakers, were descended from certain trees in the Ampadad forest, a forest whose name means "Place Where the People Are Born."

The wide commercial street was full of makeshift cloth stalls where market women and healers sold baskets, comales, clay pitchers and pots, vegetables, fruits, mushrooms, armadillo shells to hold seeds when sowing, and parasols to keep off the sun. María Sabina was striking in her thinness, her hair parted down the middle, her braids trailing down her back. She stood out with her thick eyebrows, sharp cheekbones, toothless mouth, earrings and necklaces of blue and red beads, and her habit of smoking fat cigars, drinking moonshine, and emphasizing her words and expressions with her fingers and hands.

The market was a place where people haggled over magic bundles sorcerers made containing an egg, seven scraps of brown paper, seven macaw feathers, grains of cacao, and little pieces of resin, all wrapped in a corn husk or a banana leaf. According to stories, the neighborhoods of Huautla have supernatural origins: they sprang from the ancient peaks, from the ragged hills, from the springs of rushing water, and from the trees—like the Mixteco neighborhood, which had grown out of "the tree that rises."

Heading toward her house on Cerro del Fortín, María walked with equal agility over the level streets, the steep ones, the dirt paths, the sunny and the shaded. She walked without hurrying, even though everything, above and below, within and outside of her, to the right and to the left, in the luminous hills or the clouded, was full of mystery and gloom.

She lived surrounded by the dead, those who still walked the streets, and the deceased she saw in dreams and spoke to through the mushrooms. At times she saw another María Sabina coming to meet her like a mirror image, insubstantial as the shadow under her feet. If some of the Mazatec sorcerers typically had an animal spirit, or nagual, then she had her mushrooms, her Holy Children.

Her life, which transpired between green-blue mountains the color of tranquil emeralds, was besieged by poverty and violence. A violence so sudden and deadly that even the local bands, composed largely of wind instruments, sang about all the slaughtered husbands.

"Where does the sun rise?" the teacher, Miss Herlinda, asked her students seated in hollowed logs and little chairs in the classroom.

"In the east."

"And where does it set?"

"The sun goes to sleep in Huautla," they answered.

María Sabina had built her current house herself. It had adobe outer walls and a corrugated tin roof covering interior wooden walls and a thatched-grass ceiling—remnants of a former house that had burned down mysteriously. It had two doors, one in the front and one in the back, and two levels, because of the incline of the land.

The furniture was simple: benches of hollowed-out trunks and small chairs to sit on, a wooden table at which to eat, and palm-fiber mats on the floor to sleep on. The kitchen was also basic: a clay stove propped up on three stones over the tamped-down earth; pots and *cazuelas*; a metate and a comal for tortillas, the masa formed by hand by her daughter Apolonia; cups and plates of both clay and enameled metal.

Before moving into her new home, María Sabina had buried cacao and coffee beans, eggs, chickens, and rooster feet in the fireplace. She had cooked a stew of white mushrooms with hen meat, similar to the one she liked to serve to the foreign mycologists who visited her or to local friends who would come to her house to play her psaltery. She had been drawn to the instrument ever since the Holy Children had asked her during a velada, "Do you own a psaltery?" "No, I don't." "Buy one." Later she had to sell it for lack of money; the instrument had been as dear as a child to her.

Seated on the front step to her shack, María Sabina watched the town at her feet: the main street, the alleyways spilling through the ravines, the plots of corn and beans that she farmed with her own hoe and a curved machete. With longing she stared at the Cerro de la Adoración, waiting for the arrival of the Sacred Man, that radiant figure that she had seen one night descending from the mountains on a white horse. Not far from her dwelling was the Field of the Frightened Child, a cornfield where a lightning bolt had struck a cliff and a child had seen a goblin running off toward Cerro Rabón. The oak next to her house with its twisted branches and drooping boughs was a part of her family. It had just barely been saved from woodcutters who had still managed to damage its roots. On its trunk were carved two eyes as amber colored as one of the Holy Children mushrooms. The oak, according to her, was the pride of the supernatural world, because only God could make a tree so beautiful.

María Sabina spoke to her oak: "Old friend, now that people are beginning to die, who will remember when you were young and lightning almost pulled you out by the roots? Most of my life has passed, my house remains empty, but you've accompanied me through the years with your deep silence. When I touch your trunk, I hear your breathing and your voice. Sometimes I feel that we speak the same language, the same absence. Through your branches, your ground, your sky, I've seen the world. I've seen myself."

When she spoke to others her voice was so inaudible it seemed as if she was straining to listen to herself. When she headed into town, she descended the stairs so lightly that her feet barely grazed the stones. Her gaunt face set against the gusts of wind, she kept her lips clenched so it wouldn't tear the cigar from her mouth.

"Goodbye, María Sabina," the teacher Miss Herlinda, surrounded by children dressed in muslin, called from the second floor of the school building when she saw her coming down the main street. And María Sabina, her face a fist of silence, raised her head for a moment and then continued on her way toward Cerro del Fortín.

In Mazatec, the word *book* doesn't exist, but in its litanies, like the ancient painted codices, the images showed a world where everything spoke, everything occurred, and every future was a memory. It was a world that spoke through itself, narrating snippets of history and episodes in the supernatural lives of the masters of the hills. To understand the images you had to ingest the mushrooms, *Psilocybe caerulescens*, the "landslide" mushroom, the San Isidros, and *los pajaritos*, the little birds. Praised by the ancient Teochichimeca for their virtues, they were her family, her protectors, her friends.

"I am not a healer; I don't cure using strange herbs. I cure with language, nothing more," she asserted. Then during the velada, dancing and clapping, she sang:

Our holy woman
Our woman of light
Our spirit woman
Our spirit woman

2

THE HOLY CHILDREN

María Sabina didn't know her own age. It couldn't be substantiated with official documents, or calendars, or even the memories of others—as they themselves were uncertain of their own dates. One day was like another for her (apart from births, deaths, or natural disasters). The names of the months were interchangeable, once past just something to forget. The past years were approximations, the future years ciphers for unremembering.

She and her sister, María Ana, had experienced hunger and deprivation when they were girls. They'd slept in their clothes on cold, thin mats on dirt floors. Her parents were so poor they lived in a shack with walls of mud-plastered reeds roofed with sugarcane leaves. Their father had condemned them to a life of misery, so their mother took them to live with her parents, who were so poverty-stricken that they made the girls raise silkworms and work in the fields.

"I've suffered because of my poverty. My hands are hardened from heavy work. My feet are calloused. I've never worn shoes. Walking on muddy and stony roads has toughened my feet," she later revealed. This poverty was inherited. Her ancestors had passed it on to her, and she would pass it on to her children. Deprivation and injustice were her companions from childhood through her youth and adulthood, and they had hardened her.

"I arrived at old age destitute. I had no money to cure myself. I earned a little in my store selling huipiles, aguardiente, and coffee," she often said. "I am a member of the class exploited by the National Corruption Party.* I suffered from poverty, but not misery, because I was never miserable.

"My sister and I minded the chickens and goats on the mountainsides so that sparrow hawks and foxes didn't eat them. One day when we were sitting under a tree I found, just within reach of my hand, those mushrooms that grew in pastures, ravines, and dead trees. The ones our grandparents called Little Things, Little Angels, and Holy Children. We were hungry, so my sister and I put them in our mouths and chewed them. Their flavor was bitter; they tasted of roots and earth. We felt dizzy, a little drunk, and we began to cry. The mushrooms spoke to us, and we heard their voice, a sweet voice that came from another world. I felt that everything around me was God.

"My grandfather and my mother, seeing we were on mushrooms, lifted us up and carried us in their arms while we sang, and laughed, and cried. They didn't scold us because they knew that we were glad to have eaten the God Meat.

"From then on, whenever we felt hungry and cold, we ate them. We heard voices. We had visions. Later I found out that they granted wisdom and cured illness and that our people had been taking them for a long time because they held power. They were the blood of Christ.

"One day when I was fourteen, my mother, without consulting me, gathered my clothing together and gave me to a twenty-year-old man, Serapio Martínez, who sold red and black thread for embroidering huipiles. She said, 'You no longer are mine; you belong to this young

*A play on an earlier name of the Partido Revolucionario Institucional (PRI), the Partido Nacional Revolucionario (PNR).

man who will be your husband. Go with him and take good care of him, you're a young woman now. This is how it is.'

"He didn't drink aguardiente that often, but he was a womanizer. One day he left to be a soldier and returned after eight months with some sluts who came to live in the house. He died of the wind sickness, which he had contracted in the Tierra Caliente.* He left me three children: Aurelio, Viviana, and Apolonia.

"Widowed, I grew corn and beans to support myself. I planted coffee trees. I brought pots from Teotitlán to sell on Sundays in the market. Because I had pains in my stomach and hips, I turned to the Holy Children.

"Twelve years I lived alone, until I married Marcial Carrera, a healer and a drunk who made spells out of turkey eggs and macaw feathers. I had six children with him. All of them, except Aurora, died of sickness or were murdered. Then he became involved with a married woman, so her sons beat him, attacked him with machetes, and left him to bleed out on the road.

"During this time, I began to realize that though María Ana and I were sisters, we were not the same. That even though we were both taking the mushrooms, having the same visions, and speaking through the Holy Children, they did not reveal the same secrets to us: the secrets hidden in the Great Book they showed only to me."

Like a memory of what was going to happen, one morning when they were both on the mountainside, María Sabina saw María Ana fall to the ground, where she lay as still as a black rock. María Ana was so sick the healer was unable to help her with medicinal herbs and magical rites. Unwilling to let her die, María Sabina returned to the Teonanácatl, the mushrooms called God Meat by the ancient Mexicans. She turned to them, not as a healer, but rather as the Woman Who Knows. The mushrooms would give her wisdom, and the wisdom was language,

---

*Literally, "Hot Land." This is a reference to a geographical area and tropical temperate zone in the south of Mexico.

language that resided in the book that the Principal Beings gave her through the power of the Holy Children. With their help, she cured her sister. In a ceremony she ate more than thirty pairs of landslide mushrooms, and to her sister she gave three pairs gathered under the new moon. Encircled by candles of pure beeswax, Madonna lilies, and gladiolas, she burned copal in a brazier and perfumed the Holy Children in its incense. She appealed to them: "I will take your blood. I will take your heart. My conscience is pure; it is clean like yours. Give me the truth. Come to me, Saint Peter and Saint Paul." She extinguished the candles because darkness makes a good backdrop for visions.

The book vanished. And Chicón Nindó appeared mounted on a white horse: the master of the mountains, the one who charms the spirits and heals the sick, he to whom the healers offer coins and cacao grains. He approached her shack. She saw him from inside the house, through the walls, because her eyes could see through them, and she went outside to meet him. Under his white sombrero his face was like a shadow, his being covered by a transparent aura. Chicón Nindó left in the direction of his dwelling on Nindó Tocoxho, the Cerro de la Adoración. He had come because she had called him. She was his neighbor, as she lived on Cerro del Fortín.

When the sun rose, María Sabina touched her body, the ground, and the walls to assure herself that she had returned to the world of the living. The Principal Beings had disappeared. María Ana was asleep. María Sabina knew that while she was dancing the Holy Children had been working on her body. She saw that without realizing it she had pulled down chunks of the mud and reed walls. María Sabina said, "Language makes the dying return to life. The sick recover their health when they hear the words taught by the Holy Children. There is no mortal who can teach this language, the perfect word, the language of God.... The spirit is what gets sick.... The healers don't know that the visions of the Holy Children reveal the origin of the malady."

From deep within her sister, blood and water flowed, curing her. Woken from the trance, María Sabina noticed that the hens and goats that had wandered out of sight on the mountainside had returned and that María Ana, raising herself from the ground, was walking by her side, whole. And so she sang:

I am the medicine woman
I am the prostrate woman
I am the language woman
I am the woman who swims the sacred

3

THE BOOK OF THE PRINCIPAL BEINGS

"I learned their language from no one," María Sabina swore. "The old one, Teonanácatl, the God Meat, as it was known to the ancients, revealed the secret to me in a trance. Then once the Holy Children were speaking inside my body, they took me to visit the world that has passed, where everything was seen and everything was dissolving.

"The Holy Children, transformed into Principal Beings, placed an open book on my table that grew and grew until it was the size of a person.

"This book of resplendent brightness held signs, letters, animal shapes, drawings of peyote, magic mushrooms, and mandrakes on its pages. It was *The Book of the Principal Beings*.

"I could see it, but I couldn't touch it. I stroked it with my hands, but I couldn't feel it. Its endpapers at the beginning and the end revealed and hid a world beyond our own, a world close but far; visible, but invisible; it explained that God is alive, but he is dead, that the spirits and the saints are everywhere and nowhere; that the world is always speaking to us, that every single thing has its own language, transmitted through an inscrutable silence.

"It is said in *The Book of the Principal Beings* that the sacred mushrooms express themselves in a way we can understand, without being able to understand everything; that when we make a trip they accompany us, though in reality at the outset, during, and at the end of the journey they leave us all alone.

"One of the Principal Beings told me: 'María, this is *the book of wisdom, the book of language*. Everything that is written here is yours.'

"'I accept it,' I said. 'I am a midwife, but that is not my profession; I am a daughter of God, and I was chosen to be the priestess of the mushrooms. I am the one who speaks with him and with Benito Juárez; beginning in my mother's belly, I am the wise woman, I am the woman of the winds, the water, the pathways. I am known in the sky, I am the doctor woman.'

"'Beyond the pages closed and opened among the tombstones within me, beyond the words awake and sleeping within and outside of myself, beyond the fugitive feelings flowing like air, like waters both foreign and my own, *the book* goes on,' said a Principal Being who was there but not there, who was outside and within their body, who was present there and elsewhere—because to have a sense of what was close and far away, one only had to see his eyes opening and closing.

"Who are the Principal Beings?" she asked herself. "They could be the masters of the hills, the winds, the rivers, of the caves and the springs. They could be our ancestors and our descendants, the beings that live visible and invisible on Earth, that exist how we once existed or want to exist," she said, smoking a cigar while sitting on her mat. She rose and put the book on the table that served as an altar, encircled by wax candles, lilies, and gladiolas, and for a few moments she remained silent. She burned copal in a brazier, perfuming the mushrooms that she had laid out on a banana leaf used as a plate. She brought them to her mouth and chewed them. Eyelids heavy, she clapped her hands, a wedding band glowing on one finger. The words dragged as if it was the mushrooms speaking:

Mh, mh, mh, mh
I come with everything
I bring my thirteen sparrow hawks
I know how to drink and I know how to smoke
In the form the malignant want
I will fight
Only we who walk on this road
know how the world really is

Language is wise
The book does not lie
Santo, santo santo
I am the spirit woman

4

THE CEREMONY

María Sabina woke when the night dawned, still dressed in the huipil she had gone to sleep in. Smoking a cigar, she lit a candle and carried it in her hand to place on the altar in front of the saints, murmuring, *Hmm, hmm, hmm, hmm.*

The priestess of the hallucinogenic mushrooms wasn't the only one sleeping into the evening. In the other room, her daughter Apolonia and the other local mushroom foragers who had participated in the velada were still lying on mats. The foreigner mycologists had left to go to the boardinghouse of Miss Herlinda, the teacher, so as to keep sleeping their dreams of the landslide mushrooms.

Rising when the sun set, María Sabina went to the kitchen to boil a pot of coffee on the stove. She drank it in sips from her blue enameled cup, strewn with tiny white dots like stars. From the floor the wild dog she had found in the market looked at her with devoted eyes.

"Dogs are like people—they're part of us. The problem is that inevitably they die on us," she had once told Tatiana, the mycologist Nicholas Gordon's wife.

Even though night was falling, she went out to the farmyard to look at the eyes of the flowers and the inclinations of their stalks to see what dreams they'd had. Some of them hung their heads in sleep.

"Plants have eyes in their leaves, and when we draw near to them they watch us." She brought the flame of her candle close to one plant that stretched its shadowy cells in the direction of the fire. And just like a doctor listening to a patient's chest, she felt for a wound on its stalk and found the mark of the parasite at its root.

"I am like a mountain cactus. My appearance of skeletal succulence stems from the accumulation of light waves in my weft, but the color of my body comes from the shine of the moon and the heat of the sun." María Sabina returned to her shack. Her eyes were sunk in her face because of the Holy Children.

Every Thursday, Nicholas Gordon climbed the steep road leading to her house. Sweaty and panting, he kept his eyes on Cerro del Fortín and the end of his exertions. A few meters behind, his wife, Tatiana, and daughter Ivanna struggled to catch up with him. They were accompanied by the mycologist Roger Hofmann, the director of the National Museum of Natural History of France, who was searching for the psilocybin formula for Sandoz Laboratories in Basel, Switzerland, and Richard Stevenson, the New York society photographer in charge of visual education at the Brearley School, hired by Gordon for this magic mushroom expedition. The group was anxious to participate in a rite that seemingly happened not only in this time, but also in the distant past. "For the first time the word *ecstasy* achieves its true meaning," Gordon had said.

"This is the path," María Sabina greeted the mycologists at the door of her shack. On the table altar was a retablo of Santo Niño de Atocha dressed in the clothes of a European sovereign, his head covered with a red hat and encircled with a luminous halo, a basket in his right hand symbolizing power. To the side of him hung an image of San Isidro Labrador, the patron saint of Madrid, who had given his name to one of the mushrooms that emerged from out of the excrement left by a herd of oxen on the ground. At the edges of the arroyos and cliffs, this *si*^{3} *tho*^{3} mushroom grew, "the one which blooms from the blood of Christ that Mary was unable to collect"; "the one which comes from itself, no one knows from where, like the wind that comes from who knows where nor why."

Nicholas Gordon sat in a seat leaned up against the wall. With a stubbly beard and wearing jeans, a white shirt, a rain jacket, and rubber boots for all of the mud, a flashlight hanging from his shoulder, he held the white cup with his ration of mushrooms given to him by the healer. Shaken intermittently by the visions and the turnings of the mushrooms in his body, he opened and closed his eyes, giving himself completely over to the powers of the gods. The velada was not performed for a price per se, but for whatever payment you were willing to give—a generous tip deposited into the leathery hands of the sibyl. Under the protection of the darkness, she began the night with expressions of humility; once the power of the mushrooms had taken hold of her, she jumped around, clapping, dancing, and speaking assertions of equality with the invisible beings in the Mazatec language.

Her son Aurelio sprawled out on a mat, one eye rolling in ecstasy because of the mushrooms he had ingested, murmuring to those present that the mushrooms spoke through his mother's mouth. "The mushroom itself speaks, is speech, it speaks of God, of things, of the future, of life, and of death."

"Do they all have the same effect?" asked Tatiana.

"The smaller ones are more valuable." Aurelio slurred his words.

"How did they come to be?"

"When Our Lord wandered through the country, he spit, and every time he spit, a mushroom was born. They're meaty, they have caps like hats the color of earth, and they look like dancing phalluses. They are considered divine mushrooms that hold the power of divination. We call them Little Angels because they are enchanting and entrancing. When people eat them, they lose their minds. They ascend to heaven in their visions, or they fall into a pit of deep depression."

When María Sabina seated herself at the table altar, the ceremony began. The healer perfumed the mushrooms in the smoke of the copal burning in the brazier and placed them in pairs into the hands of the participants. She warned them not to trespass into the corner of the room to the left of the table because that was where the Holy Spirit would appear. Apolonia snuffed out the candles. María Sabina, mumbling, *Hmm, hmhmhmhm,* invited the Holy Children with invocations to reveal themselves.

I am space woman
I am day woman
I am light woman
I am woman of the enchanted place

I am woman trumpet
I am woman drum
I am woman violin
I am woman music

The mycologists, stretched out on mats or sitting in chairs, observed from the shadows. They saw by the light of the moon that there were two shadows protecting the body of the shaman. Gordon recorded her words, and Stevenson photographed her face, attempting to capture her imploring, adoring movements, her arms vibrating like the wings of a hummingbird. Roger Hofmann took notes for his research, bewildered by the effects of the ingested mushrooms, each holding its own power. Tatiana watched the wooden chair burn as if a mental fire was consuming it. She feared that the flames would reach the other room and spread to cover Ivanna. María Sabina's speech became song, her manifestations ending with a *tsotsotsotso*:

Before the dark green
Before your white shadow
My silence falls like a breath
Like a drop of water

5

PHILIP AND BARBARA

Philip began, "At the end of the Korean War—not the end of all wars, we soon started another—my father departed for Sicily, apparently to find his ancestral homeland, and left my mother in San Francisco in charge of our pasta store. A few months later, a little before Thanksgiving, he called and asked to speak to me. I was sick with tonsillitis, so I played the part of a mute during the call. He told me that he found himself on the beaches of Ostia sharing his life with his Roman friend Pier Paolo Pasolini, a writer who would go on to publish the novel *Ragazzi di vita* in 1955. His news didn't matter much to my mother; she already knew about his sexual inclinations. At an academy in Oakland where she took modern dance classes, she met an African American drummer, Goliath, who, after a short introduction, moved into the house and took over the role of my father, particularly in regard to the bed and the oversight of finances. Dressed or undressed, they listened to Charlie Parker records from Thursday night to Sunday morning, only interrupting their reverie to visit the fridge in search of beer or hamburgers. They left the bed with the sheets in disarray and the floor strewn with ashtrays filled with cigarette butts and marijuana joints."

"My parents sent me to Barnard College, where Joan Vollmer had studied. She was killed in Mexico in 1951, shot in the head while her husband was playing William Tell," said Barbara. "As a teenager I helped throw Joan's parties at the East End Bar. Her apartment on the Upper West Side was a gathering spot for writers, call girls, and drug addicts. That's where I met Edie Parker, her roommate at Barnard and later Kerouac's wife."

"Jack made an appearance at the Six Gallery in October of 1955 at the birth of the San Francisco renaissance. That night he read a poem written on onionskin paper, and my Italian American poet look made an impression on him. He told me I looked like a young priest. I was depressed and started to travel. I came to Mexico to look for ecstatic experiences, but I only glimpsed the dark shapes of some demons that lived in the Pyramid of the Sun. They deported me, but I came back, perhaps out of love for Coatlicue, the goddess of frustrations."

"I'm going to close my eyes and take a nap." Barbara arranged her hair over her eyes like a mask and leaned against the window. Philip noticed the bus driver nodding off and, fearing that he would also fall asleep and take his human cargo to the underworld along with him, went over to ask how many hours more before they arrived at Huautla.

It had been one week since they met at El Gato Rojo, a dive bar on calle Río Nazas where, by the light of candles on the tables, they listened incessantly to the jazz record *Bird and Diz* and smoked weed. Philip lived on calle Oslo in the Zona Rosa, and one night he ran into Barbara, who had just arrived from New York to take a summer course at Mexico City College. She was boarding at Casa Chávez, Río Lerma number 26. After a brief conversation across their tables, they went to eat dinner at Café de Tacuba. On the street, she told him that she had studied comparative literature at Columbia University, and he told her he wrote poetry. They planned a trip to the volcano Paricutín and headed to the Buenavista station to take the night train to Uruapan. They rented a berth and went to sleep, but upon waking the following morning they found that the train had not moved at all. It lay in repose at the station like a metal lizard; they had spent the night among dozens of delayed trains. Since they had not eaten, they watched the brilliance of the sun on the structure covering the platform in a sleepy fog. And when they searched for a lighted notice board listing the next departure, they couldn't find one. They would be lucky to leave several hours from now. They were given the explanation that the train that would take them to their destination was detained in the middle of nowhere waiting for a train coming from the opposite direction with its cargo of passengers, delayed mail, sacks of corn, and pigs for slaughtering. "To Unite and Serve" read the slogan of the National Railways of Mexico. They canceled their tickets and decided to leave that same day on a second-class bus to Huautla and sleep wherever they ended up at night. They would check into the Hotel Grande. And they would search for María Sabina.

When they arrived, a green darkness covered the tiny village perched in the hills. The main road was a long vertical snake like a vision of the god of the smoking mirror. Philip and Barbara, disconcerted by their hopeless trip, looked for other humans, but the only thing that approached them was a turkey wandering between the buses. It resembled Huexolotl, the ninth of the thirteen mythic birds, the lords of the hours of the day. With a wattle crown and eyelids that closed from the bottom upward, it stared at them. Philip, who had read that this terrible bird had been charged by the lord of thunder to change humans into turkeys and for this reason there were some people who died with grains in their throat, grabbed Barbara by the arm to get away.

In the terminal the porters didn't offer to help them, though they didn't need it. Their effects were limited to some books and a few clothes in a suitcase. Dawn broke, and a sun with no heat rose over the mountains while below a bluish cold sank into the bones. A group of Mazatec women climbed into a dilapidated car that had come to collect them. With flat backsides and flat chests, they seemed lacking in both sensuality and ego. They were like living silence. Which is how they disappeared, shadows in the early morning mist.

Desperate for sleep, the pair were irritated by the peculiar streets, the ravines, and the underbrush that spilled over the precipices. A passive-aggressive mood permeated the journey, surreal as the mushrooms of

María Sabina, as if any moment the coffee plantations, the cornfields, and the mountain peaks could take on a life of their own.

They had just exited the squalid terminal when the bus that had brought them took off toward Teotitlán del Camino, continuing on its cold, rainy, and windy route. The fog swallowed the bus completely, amplifying the melancholy of the small village and the layer of clouds covering the mountain range. The women in braids and huipiles and the men in woven palm sombreros and white suits who had boarded that morning seemed like travelers to the underworld, just glimpsed through the broken bus windows.

"Can I take you to the Hotel Grande?" offered the taxi driver.

"How much?" asked Philip.

"Whatever you would be kind enough to give."

They climbed in, resembling nothing more than two clueless foreigners handing themselves over to the unknown. A patrol car began to follow them. Two policemen, one fat and the other thin, watched them with faces of outlaws. A barefoot boy, with a torn shirt and ragged pants, tried to sell them the first prize in the lottery that was to be drawn on Friday.

"I don't buy money," said Philip.

"Buy a little something for me," begged the boy while his sister, listless and emaciated, sang, "Something that makes me laugh till I hurt, Pancho Villa without a shirt."

6

THE HOTEL GRANDE

The first thing Philip and Barbara saw outside the Hotel Grande on the edge of Huautla de Jiménez was a creek sweeping along boxes of Mexican cigarettes—Tigres, Alas, Faros—as if the water itself was an avid smoker.

Leaning against the counter in reception, Philip glanced at the wall, where there was a large photo captioned "CYD CHARISSE OF THE GOLDEN LEGS."

"Do you have a reservation?" asked the hotelier with a marked Spanish accent.

"For a few nights."

"Decide how many now. We have a waiting list."

"OK."

Two teenage Mazatec girls watched Philip. They looked like wax figures that seemed to burn from within without melting.

"My concubines: Casimira and Delfina," declared the hotelier. "They're mine."

Philip looked at them intently.

"They're loose as rabbits."

"The man is jealous, don't look at them," advised Barbara.

"Baggage?" asked the hotelier.

"Baudelaire's *Les fleurs du mal.*"

"I said suitcases."

"None." Philip watched Cyd Charisse move in her portrait. She parted the purple satin to reveal a red scar that ran from her belly to her thighs.

"You pay up front."

"OK." Philip looked out of the corner of his eye at the dance star like it was a nightmarish vision, perhaps brought on by the quesadilla that he had eaten on the street on the way over.

"It's a gloomy day, but the sun will come out shortly. I am José Venancio. When you address me don't forget the don."

"OK."

"Reason for your visit?" The hotelier wrote their date of arrival in a notebook.

"To see María Sabina."

"Hmm."

"Do you know her?"

"Druggy gringos and stupid *chilangos* come from the city to seek her out so she'll cure them of being completely out of their gourds or having certain genital ailments. She makes them believe that cancer, blood disorders, depression, and any other illness will disappear with mushrooms and chants. Don't put your faith in her, Huautla is full of sorcerers and healers."

"She was recommended to us by friends."

"In town there are two houses for the insane, one for hallucinating shamans and other for castrated healers. All of them live hand to mouth, without pensions and without medical care. Female volunteers take care of them, Miss Pike and the teacher Herlinda among them. Neither of the houses are visited by María Sabina. She's afraid that she'll catch bad spirits contagiously."

"Could you give us a room?" snapped Barbara.

"Twenty-two." The hotelier handed over the key. "Casimira and Delfina will accompany you."

"What a trip." To Philip's astonishment. the actress Cyd Charisse opened her cape completely and bared her carved-up body.

"Note the sign."

The sign read: "Don't make fires, the floors can burn. Don't speak loudly, ears can't be trusted."

In the hallway, Casimira placed an overcoat on Philip's shoulders, "for the cold."

"Hay for your horse?" asked Delfina.

"I don't have one."

"If you need us, just call." The two of them left.

"Mysterium Tremendum": in the room a guest had carved this phrase over the door. On the bed was a printed sheet of paper. Barbara read: "'The holy can sink to an almost grisly horror and shuddering . . . in the presence of that which is a mystery inexpressibly and above all creatures.' Do you know this book?"

"*The Idea of the Holy* by Rudolf Otto."

"Did you need me?" The hotelier appeared at the door. Casimira and Delfina peered out from behind him, their chests covered by rebozos. "In Spain I was an anarchist, but in Mazatec-land I sleep with the flag of the republic."

"We didn't call you."

"I came to make my inspections."

"And the young ladies?" asked Philip.

"Casimira is the receptionist and Delfina, the chambermaid. Whatever you need, they can get you."

"Who left this paper on the bed?"

"One John Lennon, who spent his afternoons listening to jazz records on the patio."

"I didn't know he stayed at this hotel."

"He came with a Benedictine monk defector from a monastery in Cuernavaca, who listened obsessively to 'Gloria in Excelsis Deo' by Vivaldi while facing the Cerro de la Adoración."

"Are you sure it was John Lennon?"

"As sure as I'm looking at you now. I also remember his woman taking midnight baths naked."

"Do remember her name?"

"She formed a chorus of mermaids with my concubines in the puddle we call a swimming pool. Using her tits as flotation devices and her ass like a fishtail, they sang together at dusk in the nude: 'We are the mermaids of Liverpool / We make up the band of Quarrymen / Love me, love me smart boy / We're the mermaids of Liverpool.'"

"You mentioned a Benedictine monk?"

"He was Nicaraguan Communist wanted by Anastasio Somoza for writing a limerick about him. He found refuge in Gregorio Lemercier's monastery, that joke of a prior who sent the seminarians who wanted to be priests to be psychoanalyzed and discovered they had no vocation because they hated people and liked money and gay sex. The Nicaraguan was named Ernesto Madrigal. He was always fucking off, all the time asking: 'Where is Mitla? Is it true that that's where the entrance to the underworld is?' Fuck, that same joker described the curves of a blade of grass as lovingly as if they were a woman's and said that the trees were dressed in green suits in the summer. In the afternoons he would sit in the cornfields, a chessboard on a rock to play himself versus himself, saying that one player was José Raúl Capablanca and the other Ernesto Capablanca, or that one was Somoza and the other Allen Dulles, the head of the CIA. Fuck. At night, after eating hallucinogenic mushrooms, he would go down to the town in his underwear and talk with the angelic birds that roosted in the clock tower and that only he saw because he was a Trappist monk. Fuck."

"What happened with the monk?"

"When Lennon left to search for the God Meat, I think he fell into the bottomless waters of the Huatla caves, because he was never seen again. He left the hotel without paying his bill."

7

JOHN LENNON

Day after day the beatniks began arriving to town. At dawn you would see them crossing the fields, sitting on rocks, or sticking their heads up above the brush like aliens. At dusk they wandered all over the streets smoking marijuana, chasing off the scavenging vultures, or reciting poems to the cornstalks. They walked through the main street with mushrooms wrapped in banana leaves, or rags, or newspaper, but the stalks and caps of the hallucinogens stuck out. Those who feared that the police would confiscate them would hide the mushrooms in their clothes. They carried them with veneration, as if at any moment they might come to life and talk to them.

Some walked along the edge of the river stamping on the dry leaves; others stretched up to pick oranges off the branch. Still others just wandered from place to place, like they were in a travelogue, without any fixed direction. After long sojourns they would end up returning to the exact same spot on the rough path they had taken at the outset. You would see the women at the store buying Delicados cigarettes, a kilo of coffee, or soft drinks to quench their thirst. Or you might come upon them in the cornfields making love.

Philip liked to look out from the small window of his room in the Hotel Grande to the vista of the mountain range, where he was equally dazzled by the afternoon sun or the reflections in the river water. It made him happy to turn his gaze to Cerro del Fortín and an unspecified meeting with María Sabina, to freely wander through that green labyrinth to the ceremony of revelation, where he would be welcomed as a participant, though it may have begun and ended without him.

As for John Lennon, a few of the locals swore they had seen a young man in sunglasses covering his head with a yellow wig that glowed in the night. Others testified they had run into a poor musician who had traveled to Huautla to visit María Sabina, but they didn't know where he had been staying. A local reporter believed it couldn't actually be John Lennon, but instead was a vision of the god Tezcatlipoca pretending to be the musician.

The teacher Herlinda Martínez Cid said she'd run into him in a bakery buying Oaxacan black bread. Miss Pike asserted that the rumored musician had not actually come to town; it was just a vagabond rocker. The man in question was a crazy person that talked to himself and smoked marijuana. She had seen him once in the middle of the night on the main street walking in the rain, his clothes and his sunglasses dripping. Naked under his raincoat, he had exposed his genitals to her.

María Sabina remembered that a foreigner had once appeared at her house in dark glasses, behind which she could not see his eyes. She had run into him earlier lurking around Cerro del Fortín looking for a velada at twilight, because he was awake at night and spent his days sleeping. Her daughter Apolonia said that she had heard someone at the door of her shack humming "That'll Be the Day" but she didn't know who it was.

Richard Stevenson, looking for him in all the hotels in town, had confirmed that no John Winston Lennon was registered at any of them. And a waiter was sure he'd seen an English musician in his twenties, without a nickel to his name, who was so argumentative that at the slightest provocation he began spewing insults. The man never changed his clothes, but sometimes he would appear wearing a shirt of surprisingly brilliant white. So dressed, he would go out to walk through the deserted streets or the coffee plantations until dawn. The breasts of the woman who was with him were always escaping her clothes. The musician, because of his mercurial temperament, was called "the Look Don't Touch Man." An employee remembered that one morning that same John started to sing a song in English, slapping a seemingly unbreakable Gallotone guitar with his hands. But he broke it. He mentioned that in the corridor of the hotel he found him making out with his English girlfriend, the same Cynthia, that nymph with the habit of taking nude moon baths or stripping down in the underbrush.

"The morning he left he looked at me standing in the lobby ready to carry his luggage. As if I was an orphan, he told me: 'Fathers aren't gods, they're the sons of wretches.' And then he went down into town, while Cynthia told the taxi driver to follow him along the main road and, if it was OK, to take him first to Puebla and then on to the international airport," remembered the employee.

Following in the footsteps of the absent one, Richard Stevenson photographed the room, the restaurant, and the hallway where there were signs of his presence. He took a photo of the graffiti scratched on a glass door: "We live in a world where we hide to make love and commit violence in the light of day."

Supposedly John Lennon had left a note about a velada with María Sabina on the rickety bed. Stevenson photographed it:

> I am a coffin that walks.
> My vision emanates from my ashes.
> The voice of the cacti in the hills is mine.
> The ages blend, generations melding in the past.
> A ghost, in my own unreality.
> A face, on streets of total solitude.

Next to the poem was a page from a book:

> Carne de Dios is called Teonanácatl. It's found on the plains, in pastures. Rounded head, long stalk. So bitter it scalds the mouth, so rough it burns the throat, it inebriates the intestines, makes the heart skip,

provokes idiocy and nonsense and feverish cold spells. It is only possible to eat two to three. More is insanity. They cause anxiety, anguish, enlightenment, rage, and restlessness. They make you run from other people and terrify novices and idiots. He who eats the mushrooms often has frightful visions or laughs a lot, he runs off, he hangs himself, he throws himself off great heights. They terrify those who eat them. I eat them with honey.

They say of the arrogant, the presumptuous, the overly proud, "He took mushrooms."

I eat them, I hallucinate, I see the face of the world; I touch my emptiness, I am the master of the hills, of the caves, of the waters. I am the sightless seer.

Stevenson picked up from the floor a text by the supposed Lennon. He read it. It was a prediction of his death:

A couple of weeks ago, after a pleasant overnight in Tehuacán in the state of Puebla, I made an impressive stop in Cumbres de Acultzingo, where I had a breathtaking view over the Valle de Orizaba with Citlaltépetl, the highest mountain in Mexico (18,625 feet), resplendent in the *sol*. There, climbing *la cumbre helada*, the frozen peak, guided by a man called Tobías Rocha, I listened to the voice of the *volcán*, its guttural *música*, its mute abyss.

I took a detour to Zapotitlán to see the cactus forest, a plethora of pillars, candelabras, huge barrel cacti, and green fingers pointing to the sky. Then I set off for Huautla, a small town high in the Sierra Mazateca, to see María Sabina, the high priestess of the mushrooms.

During the velada I had my future revealed: I saw myself shot by a crazy man at the entrance of a building on Central Park where I was living, when I came out of the studio with my wife, a woman who I don't know yet. I was proclaimed dead at my arrival in the Roosevelt Hospital, and crowds were waiting for me. I saw my cremation in the cemetery. I saw my ashes given to my new wife. Then, I disappeared. With María Sabina I had a premonition of my death.

Santo
Santa
Santo

8

SALON BARCELONA

Two policemen followed Philip and Barbara through the streets, taking note of the number of times that they frequented the market to get their fill of chicken with landslide mushrooms. There weren't many beatniks in Huautla, but the number of them on the paths and trails gave the opposite impression, largely because of the fact that, apart from the mycologists, few foreigners visited the town.

Philip and Barbara were searching for María Sabina, the countercultural icon. They had been to Río Santiago, where they thought she had been born, and to the mountain, where as a girl dying of hunger she had first eaten the mushrooms. They stood out to the locals with their over-the-top clothing and their mannerisms, like how they showed no shame when lying down naked in the cornfields to make love.

Barbara walked behind Philip, her lime-green sweater tied around her waist and her threadbare pants showing flashes of skin. Her earrings fell from her earlobes like little wings. He wore mirrored sunglasses that gave the impression that suns were reflected in their lenses and carried in his pocket a notebook full of jottings. He was always in a rush, he was always impatient: to walk, to write, to listen, to love, and even to eat.

In the pocket of a jacket covered in dust from all the floors he'd slept on, he carried a passport, inside of which was a photo of his second-generation Italian American face. Taken with a suit jacket and tie, it was inscribed with the words "photograph of bearer." In a satchel he carried the books of Kenneth Rexroth, *In Defense of the Earth*, Jack Kerouac, *The Subterraneans*, and Allen Ginsberg's *Howl and Other Poems*. And one of his own, *Ekstasis*. A poem, "Mysterium Mysticus Ecclesia," was wrapped in a red handkerchief.

"Hey, Mister, you're looking pretty shaggy," yelled a barber from the doorway of Salon Barcelona. "Young man, you need someone to give you a trim."

"Look where you're stepping." Philip grabbed Barbara's arm because bricklayers were working on the road.

"Hey, Mister, five pesos to buzz you." The barber continued to follow them.

"I am becoming hairy," Philip said and entered the salon.

"What are those gringo assholes doing wandering around?" said a fat policeman who was passing by.

"Where?" asked his partner, a skinny man whose mouth was twisted as if his face had been smacked by a bolt of metaphysical lightning.

"In the barbershop."

"Let's catch them with pot in their hands." The fat policeman entered the barbershop and looked down to inspect Philip, who was sitting back in the chair with his eyes closed.

"Yes?"

"To begin at the beginning, tell me what you have on you."

"Me?" asked Philip while the barber lathered his hair and slathered foam under his nose.

"It is required that you declare yourself at the town hall." The policeman waved a black pistol that looked like a toy under his eyes.

"Identify yourself," the skinny one demanded of Barbara while shooting her salacious glances in the mirror.

"I've seen you in the coffee fields—what are you looking for?" muttered the fat one.

"What are you carrying in your backpack?" the skinny policeman asked Barbara, though he was more interested in feeling up her breasts under her shawl than her answer.

"A doll that I found on the highway next to a dead dog." She bent down to take something out of her sack, and the policeman's eyes widened.

"Careful, I am becoming visible through the roads of the turquoise sun." Philip's words emerged from the foam encircling his lips.

"What's the book called?"

"*The Lives of Great Idiots*. Do you want it?"

"What else is in there?" the skinny policeman said, harassing Barbara.

"A photo of a dead dog hit by a beer truck."

"What else?"

"A memento of the dog's hide."

"Why did you come here?"

"To see María Sabina."

"The consumption of drugs is prohibited, and if that missionary Eunice Pike keeps coming up with propaganda about mushrooms, we'll kick her out of the country."

"Everything in order, young lady." The policeman gave her a quick pat down, concentrating particularly on her pear-shaped waist. "*Chau, chau.*"

"Look." Philip pointed out to Barbara a general, decorated from head to toe with Coca-Cola bottle caps, who was just passing by on the street. The general took off his jacket and headed off toward the calle del Burro, which at this hour was as silent as bougainvillea on a wall.

9

HOWARD AND GUADALUPE

Stretched out over the bodies of sheep, which they also used as pillows, Howard and Guadalupe traveled along in a freight truck they'd hitched a ride on. Idly they watched the low clouds change from rosy white to dark gray under the blinding sun while their bodies were shaken by the bumping of the truck on the highway.

Howard talked with Guadalupe about his childhood in Brooklyn on the way. His father, Homer Frankl, had been a mail carrier until the day he abandoned his family and job to become a vagrant. One night Howard had found him on the street begging, a trembling hand outstretched, for "a quarter, a quarter." He was so high that he didn't recognize his own son.

Howard had suffered the abuse of his classmates in kindergarten until he finally decided to confront the worst bully, which resulted in a beating. But the source of his greatest insecurity was Dolly, his mother. Obsessed with the death of her daughter Lolly from hydrocephalus, she had dressed him as a girl and curled his hair until he was six years old. Other relatives and neighbors, when they saw him playing with his dolls, didn't know if he was a boy or girl. He didn't know either, but at times he feared that a girl was unfurling inside of him, a girl with straight hair like his and locks that covered his forehead and his ears. This person began to inhabit his inner spaces and left him feeling like he was losing himself. And since his mother assured him that he was the reincarnation of Lolly, he began to doubt his own identity completely. Reading detective novels and walking across the Brooklyn Bridge grounded him, and on some of those walks he would imagine he was the detective Philip Marlowe, played by Humphrey Bogart, walking to meet with Vivian Rutledge, played by Lauren Bacall, and on others that he was Hart Crane en route to write *The Bridge*.

His life changed when he met Guadalupe Liu outside the City Lights bookstore in San Francisco. An unknown girl had been looking at the new arrivals in the shop window when he dropped *Howl* by Allen Ginsberg. She picked it up and saw him standing there, staring at her with a kind and steady smile. Guadalupe was the product of a transcultural relationship: her father was Chinese and owned a traditional herbal medicine shop, and her mother was descended from the Mexicans who stayed to live in California when their lands were seized by the infant American empire. She invited him to dinner in the restaurant the Terrace in the Sun, which belonged to her uncle Su Tung-P'o, and from there they went to a hotel with windows facing the Embarcadero. But in the room, Howard was not paying attention to the view; instead he threw himself on Guadalupe's naked body like a shy zealot.

In the following days they attended Beat readings in City Lights. She wore red ballerina slippers to walk on the street and high heels to walk uphill. He wore a mango-colored shirt and lavender pants. She adorned her chest with an opal necklace of the kind that bring bad luck precisely to test her good luck and let her braids fall over her breasts, visible through a transparent yellow blouse. He wore the dark sunglasses of a San Francisco stoner at night. At parties she raised her skirt so everyone could see her thighs. They were together every minute, until one Sunday afternoon they decided to leave together to "Oaksaka" in search of the God Meat.

"We went to Mehico like the Spanish friars in the sixteenth century who traveled to New Spain to convert the Indians to Christianity and gain access to Paradise," he said.

Guadalupe Liu didn't tell her uncle Su Tung-P'o about their plans. For her it was a way to get away from the world of bodegas and Chinatown restaurants and find her own path.

"When do we go?" she asked.

"Tomorrow."

"Have you always had those long curls?" she asked Howard on the freight truck headed to Huautla.

"When Lolly passed away my mother dressed me in dresses with red tulips and started to curl my hair." With an absent expression Howard looked off into the distance at the small towns perched in the hills. "Clinging to the crags, camouflaged among them, white houses appear and disappear between the valleys and ravines like a hallucination."

"There are actual children living there, how strange," exclaimed Guadalupe Liu when they passed by a hut with burros and turkeys huddled around the doorway. Out of a paneless window a girl leaned. She was naked under her huipil and had dilated eyes. Seemingly high on mushrooms, she stared intently at something that wasn't there. Farther along, agricultural workers cut grass in the field with machetes while willows resembling their reincarnated ancestors waved violently in the wind behind them.

"Name?" the immigration official in Tijuana asked Howard.

"Howard Frankenstein."

"Date of Birth?"

"1818."

"Point of origin?"

"The cemetery."

"Profession?"

"Monster."

"Reason for your trip?"

"To look for preelectric methods of creating light."

"Hmm."

The agent showed no interest in his responses as he stamped his visa.

"On the road the colors were priceless, the eyes delighted greatly in the blues of the hills as well as the spiny orbs of the nopales." While the vehicle ascended and descended, the expressive silence of the vegetation overwhelmed Howard, who was every moment more and more seduced by the undulating hills and the array of green.

"How many stones are there in those mountains?" Guadalupe asked.

"How many trees could fit in our silence?" he asked.

The freight truck ran the route from Puebla to Tehuacán to Teotitlán to Huautla, with detours to Ciudad Serdán, Ciudad Mendoza, and San José Tenango. Guadalupe was stretched out barefoot, her tennis shoes perched next to her head for fear of losing them, while underneath her fanned-out straight hair, the sheep bleated like animals in heat.

The truck carried flour sacks, boxes of beer, packages of cookies, cans of lard, Kellogg's cereals, movie poster adverts, and a 16-millimeter projector to show movies in the towns. On a sheet erected in the plaza like a screen, they projected *The Queen of the Mambo* starring María Antonieta Pons.

"Back in a sec." The porter got down to unload merchandise into a store while the driver, collecting the wads of bills in a shopping bag, leered at the rumba dancer on the screen and the women in the plaza.

"John Lennon passed through here on his way to Huautla, and now we go toward the blessed," said Howard.

"Don't worry, we're leaving now." The driver stretched his legs at the edge of an arroyo. Suddenly a downpour started, and the subsequent deluge of water soaked everyone's hair, clothes, and shoes. They couldn't see because the wipers didn't work, so the truck started weaving. The driver braked, and the porter got down to clean the glass, using his shirt like a rag.

"Four armed criminals, faces covered by balaclavas, carrying semi-automatic guns and serrated machetes, showed up at the Cruz Azul cement factory in a gray Volkswagen with license plates from the state of Puebla. They robbed the store and stole two hundred thousand pesos in cash and an Olympia typewriter." The driver stuck his head out of the window to inform them of what was being said on the radio:

"State police units have opened an investigation to find those responsible. Don't be surprised if they stop us on the highway for an inspection. Ah, here is my niece Teresita de Jesús. She attends the local elementary school. She'll ride with us from here out." The driver stopped.

"Hi, I am Teresita, I am thirteen and good girl," said a smiling, thin little girl in a high voice as she climbed up into the rear part of the truck. Her school uniform consisted of a blouse and white ankle socks, a green sweater, and black shoes. Her backpack was overflowing with notebooks and books. She sat next to Howard and kept staring at him with a fixed smile.

"I think I see a store." Guadalupe jumped out of the truck when the driver stopped at a gas station. She crossed the highway and went into a store lit only by candles and returned through the rain with bottled water, potato chips, a loaf of commercially made bread, and a thin blanket to cover them.

A few kilometers later the driver stopped the truck, saying, "Here we are." He gave Howard and Guadalupe a farewell hug. Teresita de Jesús waved goodbye while the porter worriedly watched the lightning storm heading straight toward them.

10

GABRIEL JASÓN

The Chilean poet had traveled to visit all the highest archaeological sites on the planet with the goal of reaching the zenith of Cerro Llullaillaco, the ritual destination of ancient Inca pilgrimages. From that ceremonial cemetery reaching up into the boundless sky, he thought he would be able to see not only a range of peaks so vast they exceeded the span of the eyes, but also all the death that had been and was to come.

Over several weeks, Gabriel Jasón endured hunger and vertigo as he traveled with a group of professional archaeologists to see the ice mummies up close, as well as those immaculate immensities, the mountains themselves, all from a height of 6,739 meters.

The son of Socrates Demetrios Theologos and Josefina Carbajal, Gabriel Jasón had traveled from his birthplace of Santiago to Arica, Chile, and from there to Arequipa, Peru, at the confluence of Argentina, Bolivia, and Chile. He was fully aware that the summit of Llullaillaco was higher than that of Mount McKinley, Mont Blanc, the volcano Popocatépetl, or Mount Fuji, but the cold inside and outside (which penetrated shoes, gloves, balaclavas, and clothes) was greater than the panic that the heights could incite. The deep valleys, the crags in strange formations, and the sheer abysses were overshadowed by his desire to reach those peaks where the condors nested.

He had hoped to see something glorious, even spectacular, in the cemetery of the frozen Venuses among the Andean mummies. On the glacial volcano of Sara Sara, one female ice mummy, seated on a vessel of black clay with her intestines exposed, had seemed to be hugging herself with her upper extremities. Invaluable and indescribable, she seemed a terrifying symbol of the Andes, with her upturned face, her straight hair, and her shifting eyes. Her figure, however, completely eclipsed the impression caused by another seated on a frozen peak, with a thick red tunic, fraying sandals, a crest of red feathers, and a mask of silver foil. On this mummy's right cheek one noticed a twist—she had a mouth that had chewed coca leaves—and, like a clear offering crossing centuries and human generations, a procession of tiny painted flames in vivid color approached her, while behind her, a pattern of defiant blues seemed to ascend the luminescent peaks. There is frequent terrestrial shifting at this elevated altar, but then this was a religious ancestral faith that could move worlds, as embodied by the words of Juan de Ulloa: in the Andes, the snow-peaked mountains were the principal deities.

The figure that Gabriel Jasón had longed to see, however, was that of the heretic virgin, the maid sacrificed to Pachamama, Mother Earth. With her yellow crest representing the bird of the heavens, dressed in a cape woven with reds and yellows, earflaps in the form of hooks, a mask of hammered gold, her nose split, her eyes attentive and melancholy, and a grimace typical of a coca-leaf-chewing priest of the Andes, she was so mysterious as to be irresistible. Her face was a ritual mask of a drug-induced euphoric anguish following a long pilgrimage through the mountain range in the captivity of sacrificial priests.

Gabriel Jasón had descended from the mountains through Bolivia without allowing himself to visit Lake Titicaca. In Colombia, he had become fascinated with shamanistic symbols like the yellow-billed ducks that moved across the earth, in the air, and in the water. And then in Bogotá an issue of *LIFE Magazine* from May 13, 1957, fell into his hands. The magazine contained an article, "Seeking the Magic Mushroom" by R. Gordon Wasson, a New York banker who in the Mexican mountains had participated in an ancient Indian ritual of eating strange mushrooms that produced visions. Though Wasson had given María Sabina the name Eva Méndez to protect her identity, Allan Richardson's photos documented them eating the mushrooms *Psilocybe aztecorum R. Heim* and *Psilocybe mexicana*.

Pointedly ignoring the advertisements for hair tonics, Chrysler and Lincoln automobiles, Sylvania televisions, General Electric air conditioners, Marlboro cigarettes, RCA-Whirlpool refrigerators, ketchup, and Tampax, Gabriel Jasón was fascinated by the images of the mushroom priestess. Under her supervision, Wasson, the vice president of J. P. Morgan and Co. (accompanied by his wife, Valentina, and his daughter Masha), experimented with the God Meat in a nighttime velada in a room in a hut in Huautla. Seated on chairs and lying on mats, they saw things "that brought them there where God is." María Sabina had danced, clapped, and sang:

I am star woman
I am sky woman
I am cloud woman
I am woman dew on the grass

"It seemed to me at the time like an introit to the Ancient of Days," wrote Wasson. This and the inclusion of a William Blake quote, "He who does not imagine in stronger and better lineaments, and in stronger and better light than his perishing and mortal eye can see, does not imagine at all," made Gabriel Jasón wish to join the search for the Teonanácatl.

"God Meat," he repeated over and over as he flew in an old airplane to Mexico, traveling a route of numerous airport layovers and delays.

In the Distrito Federal, on the recommendation of a taxi driver who took him into the city, he ended up in a guesthouse for Colombian students on calle Sor Juana Inés de la Cruz. His stay there was short, however, because the student parties were loud. He then moved to the Hotel Cornada, on Cinco de Mayo, where the "Consul of the Bars" had stayed, the author of *Under the Volcano*. The hotel was a modern ruin, the windows covered with metal bars constructed to keep tenants from escaping. During the night the rays of the bar sign lights shone through the busted windows, and at dawn, the glow of the morning. There was no water, hot or cold, as the pipes were broken. Over the bed a portrait of Adolfo Ruiz Cortines, the president of Mexico since 1952, haunted his insomnia. The Jefe of the Nation, his breast covered with a tricolor sash, looked like a cursed mummy. The room did have a bonus: from a hole in the floor you could see the city adrift and feel the God Meat floating just over the horizon. But then the bedbugs came, not from anywhere far, rather from just under the mattress, so he moved to a transient hotel aptly named the Northern Pass, which was cheaper and quieter. There, women of the night, with their high heels and their bouncing on the rickety beds, never let him sleep, but they did bring on dreams of nymphs with black eyes and demented satyrs.

Seeking employment, he was hired by a *lucha libre* owner to serve as a dummy opponent in the matches. "Don't make plans this Friday night. I don't know if I am going to put you in a mask or a wig. I'll call you El Elvis Loco. Or El Jaguar Azul. I haven't decided. You'll debut a bout of mask versus hair in the Arena México, the grand center of the sport of locks, muscles, tricks, and technique," said the owner upon meeting him.

He explained further: "To warm up the audience, I'll introduce you in opening fights. Your role will be to spar with the technical wresters and the brutes: El Santo, El Médico Asesino, Blue Demon, Tarzán López, and La Tonina Jackson. I'll give you your own character. I'll dress you in El Tranvía brand pants. I'll send you to get a pompadour hairstyle with stiff hair and long sideburns. You'll be courteous with your opponent but attack them furiously, dancing around them, then dragging them on the floor."

Gabriel Jasón came out in a silk robe and a guitar in his hand like he was at a rock concert. He showed off his muscles, his narrow hips, and his virile grace. To start the spectacle, the public howled, they insulted him, they took the side of his opponent, El Nakoteca. They whistled and yelled, "Bugger," "Phony," "Gringo," and "Whore." When he was thrown against the ropes, a woman in the crowd began egging on his opponent, yelling above the melee: "Blood! Give it to him where it hurts! *¡Dale en la madre!* Bust his balls! Pull out his asshole! Stick a key up his ass! Make mincemeat out of him! Kill him!" And Gabriel Jasón, with black eyes and split lips, looked around the audience for the son of a bitch who had incited such animosity against him. He was still looking when El Nakoteca dealt him a kick in the face that knocked him out.

After a month, Gabriel Jasón, trampled and broken from being chucked against the ropes in public, left the ring out of concern for his fragile ribs and his head, which he thought "the most dignified part of the body." He found a place under a staircase in a guesthouse on Cerrada de Medellín in Colonia Roma and went to work as a waiter in a café in the Zona Rosa, where they gave him the afternoon shift. But, never satisfied, he set off one Good Friday on a peyote and pitaya pilgrimage, disturbing the Catholic observances in the towns of the Zone of Silence to eat carne asada, dried beef tacos, and nopales.

11

A DARK NIGHT

Visitors arrived at María Sabina's house by following a dirt road. They crossed cloud banks on their journey through the mountains, where sorcerers and spirits were visible in the changing forms of the clouds. Plants without roots floated in the air. The velada was held on a Thursday. A table altar was pushed back against a wall and draped in a cloth covered with embroidered flowers and birds. An oil lamp illuminated San Pablo and San Pedro and a Virgen de Guadalupe. Dried corncobs hung from the roof like amber stalactites. Next to a pot of copal were coffee beans, cacao beans and corn, macaw feathers, and fourteen pairs of mushrooms in two lines of seven.

Out there over the mountains, the mists swallowed the half moon. Underneath, Huautla dissolved into the darkness. The mycologists came up from Cerro del Fortín. Outside the shack, hens chattered, roosters clucked. A turkey covered in carbuncles that spilled from his head to his breast seemed to interrogate the foreigners. They wanted to slip past him into the shack, but a hog grumbled. Inside, in the space for the rite, the final rays of light pierced the cracks in the door.

"We smoke the day. We smoke the heart of God." María Sabina exhaled as she greeted Gordon with a cigar in her mouth.

"It's cold." Apolonia put a black clay pot of atole to heat on the stove. A little girl embraced her legs. Wrapped in a rebozo, the little one listened to her mother sing all night.

"How old is she, señora?" asked Richard Stevenson, camera in hand.

"I don't know when she was born. None of my ancestors knew their ages. All I know is that my mother, María Concepción, told me that she was born in Río Santiago, the municipal center of Huautla. My father, Crisanto Feliciano, who wore a cotton shirt and short pants, died from being transformed into a turkey. The shamans and the healers could not save him. With his neck covered in red bumps and a fleshy flap of skin hanging like jowls, he departed. We suffered greatly because he left us with nothing."

At that moment Gordon's daughter and wife, Ivanna and Tatiana, arrived.

"What will see in the velada, señora?" asked the professor Roger Hofmann. He was bald, with glasses, in his fifties, and he carried a leather messenger bag for the mushrooms.

"Marvels in the dark. Sometimes you can see the Hombre de las Montañas. *¡Tso!* But you shouldn't photograph him," she warned Stevenson. "*¡Tso!* Brilliant like the day is the master of the fields. Mounted on a white horse, he wears his hair gathered over the forehead in one golden lock. *¡Tso!* Like the mist. *¡Tso!* Like the air. *¡Tso!* Like the mind," said María Sabina, as translated by the teacher Miss Herlinda.

The foreigners had arrived to Huautla a few days before, deposited at the terminal by a bus. They were boarding with the town teacher but were so eager to learn the secrets of the mushrooms that they didn't want to miss any of the shaman's movements. Not even one word. Their ignorance of the Mazatec language, her language, was no impediment as her exalted, enigmatic, and elusive singsong voice transported them to the world of the Holy Children. She administered them in pairs, male and female, as the mushrooms had a sex and if it was not respected, one could have a bad trip.

Local mushroom foragers helped with the ceremony. A healer, a mule driver, the priest of the church of San Juan Evangelista, and the mayor were all lying there on mats, hungry for visions. And she, with invocations to the saints, rooted the sickness of fear from out of their guts. She became impatient when the spirits didn't respond to her calls. Rhythmically she spoke, "*¡Tso, tso, tso! Mhmmm, hmmm, hmmmm!*

I am the woman who arrived
I am the woman who will arrive
I am the woman who was present
I am the woman who is present"

Kneeling on a serape, the holy fool summoned the Trinity and the saints. She took mushrooms out of a cardboard box, shredded them, and divided them into clay cups. Lit by candlelight, inhaling the copal smoke, and chewing the mushrooms, she hummed something incomprehensible, something that shifted and became a song. Calm, as if the words rose from ancestors invisible to the ear or eyes, she let herself be carried by the rhythm of the litany. She hovered above herself, identifying herself as "the woman who sees below the water and behind things" and "the woman who suffers." Through the ritual she transformed into the priestess of the mushrooms. Her shadow on the floor parted from her body.

I am a woman creator
I am a woman star
I am a woman moon, a woman sky
I am woman dew in the grass

"The Holy Spirit descends to the altar. The eldest mushroom forager is transported *there where God is*. The eye that feels and thinks behind closed eyelids, the eye that is separated from the body, melds with space; it sees everything without seeing anything. The mushroom speaks," the teacher Herlinda translated the words of María Sabina. The shaman accentuated her silences and facial expressions with her hands. The ancient Teonanácatl, the God Meat, by means of the trance turned her eloquent, allowed her to cure sickness and create visions.

Under the influence of the Holy Children, María Sabina clapped and danced.

I am a woman who looks toward the inside
I am woman light of day
I am woman morning star
I am woman god star

She held the silence for several moments. Later, with a strange shining in her eyes, she took up her song again:

I am a woman who yells
I am a woman who whistles
I am a woman who thunders
I am a spirit woman

7

THE BEATNIKS HAVE ARRIVED

"The beatniks have arrived," Ivanna heard Stevenson the photographer say. "On foot, in cars, in buses, and on mules, coming from New York, or San Francisco, they walk around Huautla and its surrounding areas like aliens, disliked by both the police and the locals. You find them in the plaza, in the market, in church, and in the streets, all asking the same question: 'Where is María Sabina? I want the healer to teach me enlightenment.' Because of their outward appearance and their strange clothing, the people don't respond. They look at them distrustfully and walk away."

"I've seen them wandering along those streets that begin and end in the hills," said Tatiana. "Some of them are handsome, interesting, dressed in secondhand clothes. They wander barefoot or in sandals, they wear caps or goatees, and they hide their eyes behind sunglasses with tinted black lenses so that no one notices they are walking around stoned."

"In the little shops and stands the merchants don't discuss price, as if they were doing a favor selling the strangers grasshoppers, *tlayuda* tortillas, corn tamales, bunches of squash blossoms, *pan de San José,* coffee from Huautla, and cans of sardines. The beatniks submit to the rudeness and sometimes forget their purchases on the counter. The locals are irritated by their clothes, their shoes, their customs, their self-confidence, and their gringo-ish accents. And so, intimidated, the beatniks start to feel they have no right to walk on these streets and paths, or to examine the cloths and huipiles that are shown them in the markets," said the teacher Herlinda. "A certain one called Howard was seen kneeling down before an eagle caught in a snare trap. He seemed to believe it was the eagle that had appeared in the sky at the siege of Troy carrying a bloody serpent in its talons. Its prey was a rattlesnake. Thinking it was a good omen, he set it free."

Roger said, "The other afternoon Gordon and I ran into a couple from San Francisco in Cerro del Fortín when we were out looking for specimens in the dead trunks of trees and in the pastures and in cow patties. Crossing through the byways and the cornfields, they approached us asking to see the mushrooms we were collecting that I carried in my Swiss mailbag. We showed the woman a dozen of the Little Angels, those pale, thin, phallic dancers. But she wanted to know who we were, and where we were from, and what we were doing in the town. Meanwhile, we wanted to know who they were and what they were wandering around looking for in Huautla. They responded by saying, 'The blessed.' When we turned our backs to them, they followed us for a long distance, hoping we would lead them to the house of María Sabina."

"The other day I ran into a woman—I think her name was Barbara—who was with a Chinese woman named Guadalupe Liu coming down the steep street in the direction of the market. They were sweating in the noon heat, protecting themselves from the sun with blue parasols like the ones the merchants in the market use. They were soaked, their hair unbrushed, their lips clenched in silence, sitting on their butts to descend the loose stepping stones," Gordon told them from his seat. He spoke carefully, as if he didn't want the words to irritate his inflamed throat. "They purchased palm hats and a carton of Delicados just to then remove the tobacco from the cigarettes and fill them with marijuana. Then they headed to the Hotel Grande."

"The girls wear jeans or tights with runs, orangish jackets, scarves in place of bras, and copper earrings, and their eyes are heavily made up. They don't care about walking in the rain with wet hair or that you see their legs. Some of them eat raw garlic, tacos of magic mushrooms. They smell like copal and cigarettes," shared Tatiana.

"Also like weed, sperm, and fear," exclaimed Crescencio García, the municipal president of Huautla. "A wild dog so skinny it looks like a sketch follows them through the coffee fields. They smoke marijuana on the shore of Río San Agustín, they wander throughout the pine forests with mushrooms in their hands, and they rummage around the arroyos and the fields looking for the landslide mushrooms. When María Sabina is welcoming to them, they ask questions, they want to take photos with her, they beg her to hold a velada for them. I saw that Howard on Sunday in the market. He went straight up to her, grabbed her hand, looked at her with a huge grin, and said, 'I love you.' María Sabina didn't know what to do, but he wouldn't let go of her hand."

Stevenson interrupted, "They live in the Hotel Grande, a rambling house in ruins with depressing rooms lit by depressing light bulbs, with views of depressing bathrooms and depressing corrals. If I lived in that depressing pigsty, I would die of depression."

Tatiana added, "The men sit on the stone stairs or on a stack of bricks to watch the eagle, a macaw, or a vulture soaring over the mountain peaks while their women practice free love."

Ivanna interjected, "Because they call themselves poets, they write graffiti on the walls in Spanglish:

The New Woman soy yo
La Nueva Conciencia is you
La New Age we two do
And in the bed, on the floor, and in the street
We are four gods, you, yo, and our twins.

La Nueva Visión I divine in your ojos
La Old Visión I carry on my back

En la Era de Aquarius we smoke la vida
And under the stars we are both illuminated."

Stevenson continued, "That Howard guy wrote:

Yesterday I saw my madre
Sitting in a field of flores
With her skirt raised peeing
I ran to her with los open arms
And like an Oedipus hungry de amor, I abrazo-ed her."

Ivanna said, "Some of them write questions:

Where am I? Answer me tú
Who is here? Who wants Veracruz?
Who is Nueva York?
Who is San Francisco?
¿Who am I?"

13

PAPA GRINGO, PAPA CROCODILE

At two, the students of the Benito Juárez school left with their backpacks and headed home. Taciturn and barefoot, they passed in front of the bar the Staggering Monkeys. In the doorway was Gerhart, a German pianist who lived on the outskirts of Huautla.

The last student to leave walked more quickly, Teresita de Jesús, wearing a short huipil and shoes with the tongues ripped out. She was so shy that she avoided the company of her schoolmates, and when they spoke even a word to her she would blush. Upon turning the corner of the main street, she ran into the Son of Dolores, a known killer who had confessed that he was responsible for the deaths of four people, which he claimed he carried around with him. All of the neighborhood was caught up in a siesta of indifference at that moment. The little stores were closed. The wild dogs were stretched out with their pups among the open tombs in the cemetery. Only the signs pasted to the walls of the market were awake: "Weddings on Sundays. We hire maids in exchange for room and board. Psaltery teacher gives classes at home for ten pesos per hour. Love letters written Wednesdays in the afternoon. We take First Communion photographs. Invisible mending done. We sew custom-made huipiles. Good prices. All hours."

"RESPECT YOUR CHURCH. NO PLAYING BALL HERE," said a sign written on cardboard at the foot of a stone cross at the entrance of the church of San Juan Evangelista. The Son of Dolores walked in great strides among the Mazatec youths who were kicking around a ball, ignoring the plea. Afraid of being recognized by anyone, he covered his face with his open hand. Inside the church, he disturbed two señoras by drinking the holy water from the basin and, because he liked it, he drank some more. When he left, two wild dogs barked at him, so he shooed them away with a machete. He got in a ramshackle car driven by one of his accomplices, and they took off as suddenly as a stampede.

"William," at that moment Philip called out to someone who looked like Burroughs. He recognized him by his dry expression, black clothing, cadaverous body, thin hair combed over to the right, round glasses, mouth in a tight line, suspicious movements, and hands itching to shoot something. It was him without a doubt. Because the supposed William didn't answer his greeting and was slowly getting away, Philip replayed in his mind the timeline of Burroughs's infamies. He thought about his anonymous trip to Tangier, that city where there were so many people dying of hunger that any youth could sell their services for a dollar, and how Burroughs had entered Mexico by way of Tijuana with a tourist visa and a false name. In that border city, the author of *Junky* devoted himself to the tourism of prostitution and drugs. He had spent a gruesome night in a fleabag hotel on the avenida Revolución and had taken a trip to the dirty river, whose name he wasn't interested in learning. On the following day he had bought a used Land Rover and crossed half the length of the country talking to the vultures that flew overhead in the "raw menacing pitiless Mexican blue" while obsessively humming to himself,

La cucaracha, la cucaracha
Ya no puede caminar
Porque no tiene, porque le falta
Mariguana puta que fumar

Philip pictured Burroughs stuck in the desert. He got out of the vehicle under the oppressive noon sun to grab a torn-up doll he found in a highway ditch, and then he took some needed rest after the long drive and his drug- and alcohol-induced hangover. Laid out in the back seat of the vehicle, he didn't sleep, but contemplated the tip of his big toe on his left foot for hours. The image of his wife, Joan, interrupted his contemplation, and in a cavernous voice, in a frenetic monologue, as if he had her right in front of him, he started to rave, "Joan didn't die that night, she began to live a different form of existence. No one knows if I killed her or if I gave her a second crack at life. Neither do they know if she killed herself. Who knows? No one can be sure of what happened that night. I don't know. The error of aim that caused her death playing at William Tell could have been a dirty trick of the gringo intelligence service that were following me everywhere. Remember, I aimed carefully at a distance of six feet for the very top of the glass. And then, *bang!*, I fired one shot . . . then he cried, '*No!*' And started toward her, and then he saw her hole in her temple. He kept crying in shock: '*Joan, Joan, Joan!*' . . . So her death brought me in contact with the invader, the Ugly Spirit, and forced me into this lifelong struggle, in which I have had no choice except to write my way out." Just then, he started the motor of the car, and with the face of one hallucinating, he set off into the heart of the desert.

He emerged from a hotel situated just outside of Huautla with the express intention of searching for María Sabina. "I come for a velada and to ask her if she knows the hallucinogenic yagé.* I need a double dose that will bring on horrible visions," he said. But the shaman could feel his bad vibrations just by looking at him, so she shut the door.

Other excursions that Burroughs made in Huautla were to the center of town with the intention of looking for boys to commit the act that he called "to put down an Indian boy to state or communicate action. There-I-was-putting-down-a-little-body-in-a-country-routine-for-precocious-sex."

---

*Colombian name for ayahuasca.

"Why so sad?" the author of *Junky* raised his hand to the head of a shy schoolboy with frayed pants.

"Sad? I'm not sad."

"No food, no shoes. Papa Gringo, Papa Crocodile will give you money." Burroughs caressed the boy's fingers.

"Who are you?"

"Come and play with me. Let's go to my room," said the stranger and he offered him a rag doll with a shapeless body, a puffy face, and icy blue marble eyes. "Or do you prefer a dress for your screwed mom?"

The boy looked at the stranger's cadaverous face, his putrid teeth, his yellow fingers, his lethal eyes. "NO."

"Do you like green weed or yellow weed? Or do you want liquid to inject?" The boy, trapped against the wall, felt the man's hand grab his arm.

"I don't understand."

"I'll give you fifty pesos for clenched cheeks." The predator closed off his exit; he drew close with his menacing face, threatening the boy. "A boy your age who spends a night with me wins the lottery. I'll send him home rich."

"NO." The boy escaped his relentless pursuit and ran away up the street, stopping a few times to look at him from afar.

"Come back, *pendejo*, I'm going to give you a caramel. Or do you want fifty pesos?"

Later, heading to the center of the market, Teresita de Jesús encountered the wild blue eyes of Burroughs. But what surprised her even more was that he was eating raw meat from doña Anita's food stall. Seated at a table, he attacked it like a street dog, tearing into it with fingers and teeth.

At the entrance to the market, she saw him later embrace a man in handwoven clothes, exclaiming, "I hate Abraham Lincoln."

He walked a few steps and then stopped, holding a rifle loaded with bullets in his hands, loaded with rage. He declared to everyone around him: "I hate Abraham Lincoln."

In the hub of the market, with a thick cigar in his mouth, spewing smoke, he asserted, "I hate Abraham Lincoln."

On the cobblestone street, he lifted his foot to kick a dog. "I hate Abraham Lincoln."

At the doors of the white church of San Juan Evangelista, whip in hand, like a preacher, he yelled, "I hate Abraham Lincoln and Benito Juárez, his Mexican doppelgänger."

Half-naked, grinding his teeth: "Odio a Abraham Lincoln. I don't want the wood splitter to wake."

Standing in front of the girl dressed in white who had followed him, he grabbed her by the arms, shook her, and looked her in the face, muttering in perfect Spanglish in one shot of breath: "Who knows? Not me. The older I get the less I sabe."

Because Teresita continued to look confused, Burroughs, before turning his back on her, gave her a malevolent glare and shot out the words of Rimbaud in French, from *A Season in Hell*. They sounded like a gunshot with a silencer: "Il ne faut même plus songer à cela. Je suis réellement d'outre-tombe, et pas de commissions."

14

MEXICO CITY BLUES

"How would you define yourself?" Gabriel Jasón asked Jack Kerouac.

"As the natural-born son of two incompatible lovers, the Sun and the Moon. And you?"

"Like a poor Latin American who will die under the yoke of corruption without ever having had the opportunity to take advantage of it."

That Saturday night it rained. Jack Kerouac and Gabriel Jasón wandered without umbrellas along the Alameda. On avenida Hidalgo they passed yellow streetcars and buses full of passengers hanging out of the doors. On street corners, lottery ticket vendors shouted out the mountains of possible prizes, and butchers brandishing knives chased off street dogs gnawing at the greasy paper they served the tacos on. Gabriel had been sitting outside his hotel, reading about Alexander von Humboldt's ascension of the volcano Chimborazo in June 1802, between swallows of aguardiente and tokes of marijuana, when all of a sudden he recalled that day when, in the guesthouse on Cerrada de Medellín, he had met Jack Kerouac on his way back from shopping at La Asturiana—situated on the corner of the building of apartments on calle Monterrey where years later Joan Vollmer and William S. Burroughs got high, fornicated, and fought. That afternoon when

Gabriel Jasón ran into him Kerouac had been carrying a bag of bread, Chihuahua cheese, half a papaya, and a bottle of wine for the night's dinner.

"Free!" Gabriel Jasón signaled down a taxi. He asked the driver to take them to Cerrada de Medellín, where they were staying, and where years earlier Burroughs had also lived—that writer obsessed with the carnivorous vultures wheeling under the limpid, cruel Mexico City sky.

"Here a woman is an inverted macho, and at the top of the pyramid of corruption sits Mr. President." The taxi driver pointed to a traffic officer who had pulled over a car. "The bite of bribery is the law."

"Have you eaten in the Caldos de la Tía Jesús?" Gabriel Jasón asked Jack Kerouac. "Have you seen the apartment where Bill killed Joan with one shot to the forehead during his William Tell act?"

"I've seen it."

"After Joan was buried, Bill spent thirteen days of vacation in the Black Palace of Lecumberri. He left impressed by the courtesy and the anatomy of the Mexican prisoners."

"I'm inviting you for a few tequilas and to smoke some marijuana. I have books by Joyce, Dostoyevsky, Melville, and Thomas Wolfe. Are you interested in the Beats? They're the messengers of the new consciousness and the new paganism. The sons of Coca-Cola are now the sons of the coca plant; the sons of the struggle for liberty are now slaves of the drug. Before we sold Walt Whitman to Latin America; now we sell them arms and condoms."

Over the next several nights, Kerouac spoke to Gabriel about the Beat haunts in San Francisco: the Place, Vesuvio Café, the Black Cat Café, the club the Cellar, and City Lights bookstore, where Allen Ginsberg read "Howl."

"What can you tell me about your trip?"

"It was fantastic, but in one part of the way we didn't go from east to west, rather from west to east, following the blue sky. Some things went, and some came, and now I'm a stranger without joy walking the streets of Mexico."

"Do you mind? I just watch because I'm interested in ballet." Gabriel peered through some binoculars at the antics of his Venezuelan neighbor, a dancer who collapsed every night on the table, drunk.

"You were talking about Luis Buñuel. Who is he?"

"The forgotten director of the film *Los olvidados, The Forgotten.* And of *Subida al cielo, Raised to Heaven.* If you say *Su vida al cielo* instead, *Your Life to Heaven,* the spelling error has a meaning. Afternoon after afternoon Buñuel stood in front of the window of Café Kineret to get an eyeful of the women sitting there showing their legs. Just for a moment, then immediately he disappeared."

"Someone told me about a painting in which Nahui Olin covered in eyes is looking at the thighs and black shoes of dancers on a stage, while some men in the front rows watch them with binoculars."

"That woman went crazy. In love with her father, but even more so the sun, she took off and dedicated herself to the astral king, using her eyes to conduct herself to the heavens by spinning her head. One time I saw her in La Alameda walking her angel cats. She wore one red shoe and one black. She went around half-naked, and her hair was like the rays of the sun. She liked to pose naked, baring her nipples and her pubic hair. She asked me once what Edward Weston felt when he photographed her."

"Desire."

"And what happened after she modeled for him?"

"What you imagine happened."

"What are you writing?"

"*Mexico City Blues,* some poems where I state that I want to be considered 'a jazz poet / blowing a long blues in an afternoon jam session on Sunday.'"

"Last night I wrote a love duet between the Andes and the Alps."

"Good for you. Do you like Pablo Neruda and García Lorca?"

"*Residencia en la tierra* and *Poeta en Nueva York.*"

"Want to go to Café La Habana?"

"No, let's go to the Kineret. That's the café where Arabella Árbenz goes, the daughter of the Guatemalan president ousted by the CIA. Or do you prefer to explore the darker places, the sordid neighborhoods of El Centro, like calle Violeta or calle 2 de Abril?"

"For sordid things, *me gusta* the Colonia Santa María la Redonda, that neighborhood of cabarets and holes-in-the-wall where the band Los Panchos sing boleros about love."

"Let's go to the Sanborns on Río Tíber, that's full of ladies of the night and theater vampires. Or do you want to go to Las Vizcaínas, where they exhibit country whores and laborers in the windows?"

"I prefer the brothel, La Bandida. Bill told me that they beat effeminate waiters there and shoot at drunk whores, who are so intoxicated that when dawn arrives, they no longer know who to open their legs to."

"Let's go Saturday. Sunday mornings are perfect for recovering from last night's hangover of sex, marijuana, and alcohol with orange juice and black coffee. Stretched out on my rickety bed, I don't want to get up again until Monday."

"Take me to Huautla and María Sabina to try the God Meat."

"I'll take you," promised Gabriel. Though that Friday night they went to a party thrown by the actor Dennis Hopper instead. He was renting the house of a PRI politician and, swept up in a perfect storm of cocaine, marijuana, and tequila, started breaking furniture, windows, dinnerware, and pretty much anything made of glass that reflected his face. The filmmaker Alejandro Jodorowsky tried to calm him in his destructive frenzy, but the outburst resulted in the PRI politician mobilizing the police to force the actor to pay damages. Dennis, in a moment of lucidity, caught the first plane to Los Angeles and escaped. Then, to make things worse, that following Monday Gabriel Jasón and Kerouac ran into a group of Beats in the Café Las Américas, on a stretch of avenida Juárez. The recent arrivals had taken over all the tables, filling the terrace floor with their backpacks and striking up a conversation with Philip and Barbara.

"What are you up to, muchachos?" Moshe Rosenburg came out to ask when the strong odor of marijuana permeated the café. "Just please don't smoke pot. If the police come, they'll close down the place."

"Would you like a hit?" Barbara offered him a roach that had been clenched between her yellow lips.

"Please just order some cappuccinos."

"Let's go visit the temple of official information," suggested a red-headed beatnik.

"Let's go!" The group got up and headed toward avenida Chapultepec and the Televicentro building, the headquarters of the Mexican television station.

On the way, Kerouac left them; he wanted to write. Philip and Barbara said goodbye to the beatniks on Paseo de la Reforma. Later, lost on the roundabouts, they went and refueled in the trees, trampled hedges, and then loitered outside the entrance of the París Cinema, the whole time kissing and holding each other, indifferent to the onlookers.

Barbara contorted her body like a vine. Philip stroked her with hungry hands. Langorously, passionately, they embraced. A mirror on the wall reflected them like ghost lovers walking in public, until finally they turned off onto calle Geneva. Before they got to calle Hamburgo, they slipped into a building with a pizzeria on the first floor and spent the night there in one of its rooms.

In his love haze, Philip wrote the poem "1957":

In a neighborhood in M
Where death has its altars
I saw my ex-lover in a politician's limo
Stretching her feet on a tricolor flag
Whose red was painted in blood
Fresh from a murdered woman.
By a street with melted lamps, I arrived at a hotel.
Between its walls of frozen marble
Naked girls swam in a sea of indifference.
In the lobby, with open arms and a lipless mouth
Catrina la muerte was waiting for me.

"Yesterday night, a Chilean national, Gabriel Jáson, led the scaling of the Televicentro tower against a large mobilization of the police," read the news the following day. "Gringos high on marijuana urinated from the top of Televicentro tower. With the help of officials, the longhairs were escorted down, arrested, and transported to the Miguel Shultz immigration detention center for further interrogation and deportation."

The next day Gabriel Jasón, seeing he was mentioned by name, was fearful the police would throw the book at him and blame him for the disgraceful acts. He left the city of palaces for the town of shacks and set off in search of the God Meat.

"I am leaving to witness the meeting of the defectors of abundance with the poor seekers of God," he told Kerouac.

15

GERHART MÜNCH

Out of Phlegethon!
out of Phlegethon
Gerhart
Art thou come forth out of Phlegethon?
With Buxtehude and Klages in your satchel, with the Ständebuch of
  Sachs
in yr/luggage
—not of one bird but of many

"Ezra Pound dedicated these verses to Gerhart Münch before printing his score in 'Canto LXXV' of *The Pisan Cantos*," said Vera Lawson, Gerhart's wife.

Philip and Barbara had been walking on the edge of town when they heard the sound of piano playing from one of the shacks.

"A Chopin nocturne in the middle of the day." Barbara drew closer to the narrow wooden doorway. "I wonder how they could have even fit such an instrument through this hole."

"Some Mazatec houses have two entrances, one in the front and another in back, facing the brush."

A woman with a hoarse voice opened the door. "Come in. Are you on a trip? What brings you to Huautla? Have you come to see María Sabina? She's a friend of ours. Do you prefer mezcal or aguardiente? Come sit, make yourself at home."

"We heard piano music and wanted to know who was playing," said Barbara.

"Gerhart, my husband. He can play all the livelong day." She motioned to a man in a black suit and white shirt sitting in front of an enormous Steinway piano. How they had gotten it in the small kitchen with its packed earth floor was an enigma worthy of Zeno.

"How did you find a piano of that size in this town?"

"The teacher Herlinda sold it to us. She bought it from Venancio, the hotel owner. He bought it from the orchestra director in Morelia."

"Welcome to Mazatecolandia, land of the immigrants Mickey Mouse and Mimi Apolonia." A tall man in his fifties, thin and hawk faced, rose from the bench while still playing trills. "A gringo soldier took my right eye during the occupation of Rome." He pointed at the black patch with his hand.

"Gerhart is joking. A drunk took it in a bar in Guanajuato because he didn't want to raise a glass for a toast."

"Vera lies. Since we got to Mexico, she doesn't want to know anything about the sacred Roman empire of Benito Mussolini. And I find it strange that the dictator carried the name of a Oaxacan Indian."

"What happened in Italy?"

"In that fascist country I made friends with Ezra Pound. In 1935, I met Vera Lawson on the island of Capri, and I married her in Naples two years later. Pound invited me to collaborate with Mussolini, but my relationship with Il Duce turned bitter and then fucked my career. And because Pound had been a traitor to the United States, passing anti-American messages on the fascist radio, he was thrown in jail in Pisa and labeled a black traitor."

"You forgot to mention that in 1940 you enlisted in the German army and in 1945 you survived the Allied bombing of Dresden, the city of your birth, and that you walked on foot from Dresden to the outskirts of Munich, where you proceeded to fall sick."

"How dramatic the Bostonian is being."

"Pound turned Gerhart into a fascist. Their friendship ruined him," Vera explained. "In 1947, sick of the postwar period, we left to the United States, to Big Sur, for the natural beauty."

"How did you end up in Mexico?"

"In 1953 we traveled on a freighter to Manzanillo. In a bar in Cuernavaca, I met the writer Malcolm Lowry. He was drunk and invited me to the movies to see the film *Las manos de Orlac*. Because it was a dark copy with bad sound, the film seemed gloomy. I was fascinated by the hand that played the piano, because the bloody hands of the virtuoso pianist are the hands of the killer. The theme applies to my own story, not because my hands were damaged in an accident, but because I damaged them on a daily basis, crawling up the hill to my house, paying for the sin of having been a fascist. We left the cinema and drank mezcal in a brothel until we passed out. I woke up in the street. Malcolm was gone. I never saw him again."

"How did you end up in Huautla?"

"After stays in Tacámbaro and Guanajuato."

"Does Gerhart only play Chopin?" asked Barbara.

"He also composes choral music, but when he plays he falls into a rage at the deficiencies of his audience here. Now, it's only the owls, the vultures, and the sapote trees that hear him."

"Would you like some?" Gerhart rose from the table and opened a bottle of aguardiente. Empty bottles were lined up against the wall. "For your thirst."

"Gerhart, it's early, you haven't eaten a bite since last night."

"It's the night to me. *¡Salud!* Vitamins for the liver."

"Doesn't the isolation weigh on you?" asked Barbara.

"Above and underneath this silence is so much music," said Gerhart. "Music in the stones, music in the grass and in the dust. Simple music that I've learned to dream with eyes open."

"Would you like coffee?" Vera served them some boiling water swimming with grounds.

"I suffer from acid reflux," said Philip, abstaining.

"Have you noticed the misty mountains that blot out the sky in Huautla? They are clouds, white mountains on top of green mountains, gray monsters pregnant with rain. Peaks or pineapples, rough on the outside, tender on the inside, they shine, pierced by hundreds of beams of light," emoted Vera, who was a poet.

"I want to play Scriabin's Sonata no. 4, *Prestissimo volando*, to clean out my interior grime." Gerhart began to wallop on the piano as if the night was coming frenetically out of his fingers. "Or is it time for some Chopin-azo? Have you noticed the expressive silences of nature?"

"A monarch butterfly / Flutters close to the November dahlias. / A brief resting of orange wings / On mauve / Against eternal blue." Somewhat drunk, Vera recited her verses, imitating the Boston accent of her grandfather Thomas W. Lawson, the financier who had dedicated his life to fighting against monopolies.

"Speak *castellano,* please," begged Gerhart, wringing his hands.

Two foreigners came crashing across the coffee fields, loudly, as if they were wearing steel boots. But actually they were wearing huaraches with rubber soles, like those the foreign agent Juan Rulfo went around selling. Behind them was their car, which they had abandoned at the edge of the cornfields, looking like a scarab in the sun.

"Those are our neighbors the Gestapos, Doctor Mabuse and the wicked M (who is dressed as a woman). He worked at the Drancy internment camp and he/she worked in Bucharest during the Second World War. They both appeared in the film *Germany, Year Zero* by Rossellini, lost dogs in the ruins of Berlin." Vera motioned to the corpulent man with coarse features who wore a military-type jacket and a woman, one-eyed, with broad shoulders and manly hands, who trampled through the grass in huge shoes. "It just so happened that of all the houses in the forest, they had to buy a cottage at number 66, calle Benito Juárez. It might have been a coincidence, but they didn't choose number 65 or 67, which were empty, just the one closest to us."

"Once a week, they walk several kilometers to come and speak German with me." Gerhart laughed. "We met in Dresden during the Allied bombings when we were hidden together in an air raid shelter."

"Before they came to Huautla they spent some time in Chiapas on a ranch. They helped the local governor control the Lacandon Indians, who were resisting his desecration of the jungle. They were the proprietors of a stockyard and ran a hotel frequented by Nazi fugitives. They were very eccentric; to while away the boring afternoons, they would play American football with a mamey."

"Do you have guests?" asked the man with a strong German accent.

"We don't want to disturb, but if you offered us a *copita* of mezcal, we wouldn't be angry." The woman hung her black jacket on the chair, leaving a gray hat on her head. If she was not a man, she resembled a man. If she was not a Nazi, she resembled a Nazi. She asked the beatniks, "What brings you here? I hope you aren't getting into trouble."

"Let's go." Barbara looked into the eyes of the man watching her behind thick lenses as they widened in size to take in her curves.

"Time to go, oh *abandonado*." Philip headed to the door.

"Don't go." Gerhart Münch tried to stop them. "The day starts yesterday."

16

THE BOOK OF IMAGES

In the middle of the night, Roger Hofmann showed María Sabina *The Book of Images*.

In the first photo she saw herself raising a mushroom to her mouth. Sitting on her heels, thick eyebrows, sharp cheekbones, wearing a typical huipil with flowered borders and a rebozo covering her long black braids. Everything gave the impression of having a momentum of its own, independent of her.

In the palm of her left hand, the shaman was showing the photographer a fistful of Holy Children. At her side, her son Aurelio, a boy of nineteen years, was spread out on a mat, tripping, his eyes almost shut and his face in ecstasy. He looked sick, not right, as if he was trying to draw support from her on his trip.

"How strange. It's been some time since I've seen you. Since they killed you, I've only seen you in dreams," stated María Sabina, fixing her eyes on the photo as if her son was there in bodily form.

"Mamá, I know you are going to lose me," Aurelio seemed to say, without words, with only his sadness.

"Don't say that." She tried to calm him, silently, with her eyes.

"No one is capable of holding off tragedy," he responded, his face shaken by his forebodings.

"The Holy Children will speak soon." María Sabina passed the mushrooms through the smoking copal. One by one she ate them without ceasing to look at Aurelio.

A little later, the mycologist drew near to María Sabina to show her other pages in *The Book of Images*. He placed the open book on the floor. He showed her pages of colored photos of her, taken by candlelight.

In the first image, the healer, seated on the floor, eats a mushroom while in her left hand she holds a handful of *Psilocybe mexicana*. Her shining hair is brushed with a center part, and she wears her characteristic huipil tied with blue and pink ribbons and flowers and birds embroidered on her breast. Her son Aurelio is at her side, in muslin clothing, looking at the mushrooms he holds in his hand on a white plate.

In another image, the priestess perfumes the Holy Children with copal. The bluish smoke rises from her hand up her arm and envelops the face and body of a girl under the influence of the mushrooms, who watches the scene with huge, brilliant black eyes. The eyebrows of the little girl looked just like María's.

Gordon leaned over the book on the table. To his surprise, a current of images slid off the pages toward his eyes. Pulled along by an interior river, he couldn't hold on to, or even recall, the perceptions that presented themselves to him. Like a fluid mountain range, they evaporated in his mind or dropped off into valleys of forgetting.

Attacked with drowsiness, he tried to assume control over the images, to slow them down, to memorize them. But they were lost, one replaced by another, the same and different, close by and far away. People and things changed places; they left, returned, and were extinguished. Strange situations, mundane incidents, characters from films and novels, landscapes of paintings presented themselves in a lethargic vision wrapped in a living silence.

Tatiana, weighted down by images of her sleepless life given to her by the mushrooms, seemed to suffer from a temporary amnesia. And at the same time, as a side effect of the Little Angels, she seemed predisposed to revisit unpleasant experiences in her life.

The mayor, Cayetano, sat in a corner, barely visible in the darkness. As if he was obscured by a wingless chimera, only sounds emerged, sounds that signaled he was coming out of a deep interior fog. Afterward, he approached Apolonia in the kitchen, intent on convincing her of her mother's earning potential if she were to charge tripping tourists for the veladas. "I don't know if you've seen the number of foreigners wandering around the streets looking for her. They come to city hall to ask where she lives. Some of them bring bags of marijuana, but they are hungry for visions. They offer huge amounts of pesos for private veladas."

"Some have come to see us, but we've denied them."

"They're dying to trip with your mother, to go the kingdom of bliss. If the police and military leave them alone and don't deport them, we could set up some good business."

Eyes open or shut, both inside and outside of himself, Gordon watched John, the theologian of the Zone of Silence, surrounded by circles of stones fallen from space. He wrote in the sand, not the Book of Revelation, but instead *The Book of Images*. In this book, the Babylonian whore was seated on a presidential throne on a yacht fitted with tractor wheels, driving along a highway. A necklace of diamonds adorned her breast, a crown of silver her head, and her hands were covered in emerald rings. A soldier mounted on a skeletal donkey approached her. A demon with the head of an ass delivered a speech to creeping nopal cacti. Vultures flew by. The night opened. The horizon opened. The earth opened. The ancestral sites of the Below and the Above opened. The god of the sun breathed, and the hills revealed their pyramid forms.

"The hallucination is defined by instantaneous forgettings, it is unwoven by word women, and it ends by making us drowsy," explained Hofmann.

Some of the images showed the shaman with mushrooms in her hands during a velada in 1955. The photo was taken just as she was about to eat them and conduct the attending mycologists beyond the thresholds of the vision.

"Papa, I see things," said Ivanna, seated on a wooden chair.

"Me too," answered Gordon. "In *The Book of Images,* Baudelaire's prostitute appeared in a hotel in Paris walking at dawn toward a market where sordid diners filled up on tripe and cow shit. The young prostitute carried a single cherry."

"C'était l'assassin," exclaimed Stevenson. "Crooked windows in decrepit buildings watched the killing of the prostitute from across the street. I've taken over your vision."

"I follow the path of the Son of Dolores to the house to kill Aurelio. I see Mamá's cry resounding off the stone walls of the cave of Cerro Rabón, like the killing happened somewhere else," revealed Apolonia.

"In a migrant holding station in Mexico City, I see a beatnik. He's wearing a checked shirt and a two-day-old beard, and he's being pursued by the police. He is being accused of leaving the Wells Fargo offices with bags of weed. The foreigner doesn't resist and is taken to a cell to be interrogated and deported," said Ivanna.

"In the country of the Tarahumara, Antonin Artuad ran through the mountain not like a Rarámuri but instead like a Parisian on peyote. He ran with open arms and his body in the form of a cross. At the edge of a precipice, he stopped. The landscape burned, a bonfire of green flames. There was no fire; the dancers burned in a cube of ice," Gordon described his vision.

"I surprised some beatniks making love in a coffee field. The setting sun set fire to their bodies. Afterward a rattlesnake, a *Crotalus horridus,* appeared under their legs. A rattler with huge black spots in the shape of a whip. It opened its jaws, and out came two obscene tongues. Fearful that it would attack them, the beatniks jumped up and left their clothing behind." said Ivanna, laughing. "I think their names were Howard and Guadalupe."

The face of María Sabina was a mountain range of roughness. The mouth of Tatiana, a triangle lit by the dawn wine. Gordon's double chin melted into his shirt. From Apolonia's eyes welled lonely tears of love.

"Ivanna has still not said goodbye to me, but I feel nostalgia about not seeing her tomorrow. I am going to take photos of these hideous people sleeping peacefully." Stevenson approached the sleeping mycologists and the mushroom foragers with his camera.

María Sabina, wrapped in her huipil embroidered with birds and flowers, articulated the words that she spoke in the first and third person with her hands outstretched, as if she was at once speaking as herself and as the mushrooms:

I am the woman who was born alone
I am the woman who fell alone
I am the woman who grew alone
I am solitude that died alone

"Close the doors of the vision. I can't take so many repressed images spilling out of me all at once," begged Tatiana.

"Me neither." Hofmann slammed shut *The Book of Images*.

17

GABRIEL JASÓN IN FLIGHT

"Black A, white E, red I, green U, blue O, vowels . . . O the Omega, the violet rays of its eyes." Gabriel Jasón whispered the verses into Casimira's ear as if he could impregnate her with poetry.

Over in reception José Venancio appeared suddenly, a beret on his head and a cigarette in his mouth: "Who screwed my concubine? Who touched her? Someone entered my bedroom when I was away in Teotenango del Camino and feasted on my concubines. It must have been a beatnik asshole."

"No clue," answered Philip.

"Like some sort of vampire, he got into my bed and fornicated with both of them. The fools, pretending they were asleep, pretending it was me. They let it happen. They woke up fucked and sticky and I hope not pregnant. It will be the last straw if in nine months I'm father of a bastard brat. Tell me right now, who was sleeping in my bed?"

"No idea."

"Last night, while I was unloading sacks of beans for the lunch today, some asshole appeared like a ghost to my wife, Juanita. Without a lamp or candle, he did his business with her underwear pulled down in the corral." The cook approached the table where Philip and Barbara were drinking aguardiente. "If whoever did this hides from me, I'll butcher him."

"I know nothing."

"I'm no fool!" the butcher said, brandishing his knife in front of Philip's eyes.

"The night smells like pussy. There's a hawk in the henhouse hypnotizing the unwary. If you're looking for him, you should ask me. He came in between two and four, in the afternoon and in the middle of the night." Gabriel Jasón passed by holding up his pants with his hands, as he wasn't wearing a belt.

"You owe me for dinner last night," the cook said, intercepting him.

"I left Kafka's *Metamorphosis* on the table as payment."

"Grab the beatnik!" Suddenly Philip and Barbara saw José Venancio running after Gabriel Jasón, pistol in hand.

"They go free, the horny bastards. They come out of their caves and get in the beds of our women, and our women take them for us, like idiots, just asking to get pregnant." The cook chased after him with his butcher knife.

"Don't let that pug face escape, that lecher from the mists of Ayutla," yelled a pig farmer who was on the hunt for a man who had seduced his daughter in a pigsty.

Chasing the chasers was the owner of the *tortillería* This Is Mitla. Someone had stolen his lover from him, a married woman who would roam the town with a cart at dusk, yelling, "Oaxacan tamales! Oaxacan tamales!"

"Cut off the stallion's balls! They must be size of avocados," clamored a gardener, wielding a pair of rusty scissors.

"Let's trap him," exhorted a café proprietor because a stranger had taken off his sister's panties behind city hall and made her orgasm.

In Cerro del Fortín, the town president, a healer, and a primary school teacher had all gathered to capture this stud, wielding machetes and also a shotgun. And Gabriel Jasón was on the verge of being captured by them when the mushroom priestess's door opened, offering refuge. He was lost from sight.

18

NOMADIC PROSTITUTES

On his flight from town, Gabriel Jasón encountered more women. His guide, Óscar Wilde Gómez, had offered to hide him from his persecutors by spiriting him out of Huautla, for a price. "Take me to the backwoods whores," Gabriel Jasón had asked.

"Young ones or old ones? The old ones might be older than the masks used by the dancers in the dance of the old ones."*

"Young ones."

"Do you need a mule or a mare?"

"A white mare." Gabriel Jasón mounted the animal and dug his spurs into her ribs.

"Don't poke her so hard—mares have feelings too."

His guide mounted a mule, and they started off in the dark, leaving Huautla. They crossed various bodies of water that in the middle of the night one could still identify as Río Escondido, Río Santiago, Río Tonto, Río San Lucas, Río Aguaje, or the subterranean cave that disappeared in the underground San Agustín network. They crossed

---

*A traditional dance of the Purépecha peoples in the Michoacán region, which depicts the cycle of life and is danced in homage to the old god, or the god of fire.

low hills that might have been Cerro Golondrina, Cerro Carrizo, Cerro Yeso, or Cerro de la Adoración. They traveled over stony ground, ravines, pine forests, and dirt roads to arrive at an abandoned shack with wood walls and broken windows, hidden in the town of Ninguna Parte, or No Place.

"What is this ruin called?" asked Gabriel, his heart sinking.

"It has no name—it's waiting for you to baptize it." The Chilean poet noticed for the first time that his guide's black hair had a single skunk-like white stripe, though he was very tidy looking and didn't stink at all. "It was a school before, but it had no teachers because the class was only one little girl who came there to sleep."

"And these yellow dogs stretched out around the door?"

"They're the starving and filthy dogs that adopted the girl. They stayed on to live in the rooms."

"Great company."

"*Hasta la vista*. This will be your house. You won't have bread to eat or water to drink, but all the air here is yours." The guide shrugged his shoulders as though he had an involuntary tic. The bagginess of his clothes made him seem like he had borrowed them from someone else.

"What will I do here?"

"You will see, you will say, you will know." Óscar Wilde Gòmez set off on his mule, holding the mare by the reins, until he became lost to view in the depths of the valley, like a spirit disappearing at dawn.

Swallows swooped under the roof, flying low. Or maybe they were bats, because they squealed. Gabriel Jasón entered the hovel. There was no furniture, no kitchen in the place, but after inspecting his surroundings and admiring the sunset, he figured out he could sleep on a pallet he found balanced against the wall.

During the night the cold penetrated his bones, and he felt more miserable than ever. But then he had an erotic dream where the *ahuianime** of ancient Mexico and the harlots of contemporary Mexico

*This is reference to female Aztec sex workers who ministered to soldiers and sacrificial offerings. Their name, *ahuianime*, means "happy women" in Nahuatl, so

covered his body with caresses and filled his mouth with cobwebs. He feared that he was about to die when, just like in a mushroom trance, he heard a friendly voice that seemed to belong to a Principal Being, like one of those spoken about by María Sabina, and with borrowed wings he felt transported through the air between eagles and vultures, until the creature dropped him on the ground.

"I can't believe it," said Gabriel Jasón when he discovered some women just outside at the edge of the Río Tonto. Their huipiles were hiked up, and they were using the rocks like pillows and the grass like towels. Other women splashed in the water wearing canary-yellow or parrot-green swimsuits. And some gathered in the shade of a tree, watching the highway and hoping truckers on the Huautla-Puebla route might pass or even the *tequío* cooperative workers who were building hanging bridges across the ravines. They were nomadic prostitutes. They traveled with sleeping mats and rolled serape blankets, which they laid out on top of the stones and grasses and used as improvised beds, after first shooing away the mosquitos and red ants.

A bottle of aguardiente lay at the feet of Rosa Quetzal, a Guatemalan teenager who had been captured by sex traffickers in El Petén after the CIA-sanctioned state attack on Jacobo Árbenz. Traumatized by the sexual violence she had suffered, she was always drunk and wanting to get drunker. The circles painted around her eyes like leopard spots were two deep shadows.

"I'm Juana of the Mixe," a girl with budding breasts, brushing her long hair with a toothless comb, introduced herself. Her flesh-colored tights looked like chaps. "These are my friends, Teresa the Tzeltal and Tomasa the Tehuana. The three of us like to drink aguardiente and smoke cigars. Buy us a drink."

"You a gringo?" asked Teresa the Tzeltal, who stood out with her informal dress and her hair wrapped in a red handkerchief. Perched on her breast was a green iguana with the faraway eyes of a dinosaur.

---

they are also sometimes referred to in Spanish as *alegradoras*.

"Twenty dollars," said Tomasa the Tehuana, a short-statured, curvaceous girl in her twenties, as she motioned toward a striped blue love shack. The crude dwelling was perched on a ravine, with green vines growing up its bare sides and over the gray stones. A red sign hanging from above read: "ATTENTION KLIENTS KNOC ON THE GREEN DOOR."

"Come on in, compadre," said the proprietor, El Popoluca, from inside the cantina. Also known as the lawyer or the sorcerer, El Popoluca had sharp cheekbones and a tight, mean mouth. He was an aficionado of the mambos of Dámaso Pérez Prado, and he liked to dress in white pants, patent leather shoes, and colorful vests. Frequently the cantina and the shack and even the forest would vibrate with the trumpets, the timbales, the saxophone, the trombone, the double bass, and the piano in Prado's orchestra, the same Prado also known as "Cara de Foca," or "Seal Face." In the Popoluca language, the word *hunger* doesn't exist, and to demonstrate this the owner of the bar bragged that his portions looked like they had already been eaten. He didn't hide his passion for the Cuban rumba star María Antonieta Pons, the "Queen of Mambo," and had posters of her everywhere he could hang them. "The cinema is a cabaret for everyone," said El Popoluca, who bragged he knew the dives, the bars, the jails, the police stations, and the arroyos where the most beautiful women in Oaxaca bathed, all the way from the Istmo to Puerto Escondido.

"Interesting." Gabriel Jasón headed straight to Teresa the Tzeltal to dance with her, but a little girl with huge, almond-shaped eyes ran up and intercepted him. "It must embarrass you when a stranger approaches your mother for sexual pleasure . . . ," he said, scooping her up and bouncing her in his arms.

"Thank you, señor," said Teresa gratefully. A gratefulness he took as a sign that she would be open to his advances. And so shortly afterward the two of them entered the shack to perform the act that she called "the rain dance."

The shack didn't have a bed; it had a floor of packed earth. It had no chairs and no table; it had wooden walls with knotholes through which the mountain air entered, as well as Popoluca's spying glances. It had no roof, but it had a sky, a sky in which one could see Venus hanging from the moon like a pearl.

When Gabriel removed himself from Teresa the Tzeltal's body, she watched him with such intensity that he grew fearful. The thought occurred to him that she could kill him while he slept. But she was only focused on painting her nails. Opening her purse, a coin purse, a compact, a comb, and a mirror fell out. Its gaping interior was like a black hole.

"I want to do it with you again," he told her, standing up in the doorway of the room. Her little girl was waiting outside, seated on a stone, looking faded in the sunlight. Meanwhile the music of "Mambo No. 5" echoed throughout the hills, giving a rhythm to the day, shaking everyone's bones.

"We come here only to sleep, we come here only to dream; it is not true that we come to live on earth," Popoluca whispered into the ear of Tomasa the Tehuana as he danced with her. "Be cool, beautiful, don't move your ass so much, I can't hold on to your waist with so much swaying," said El Popoluca, dancing with her like he was dancing with María Antonieta Pons.

Gabriel Jasón spent two days here, and his nights he spent eating, drinking, dancing, and hanging out with the Tehuanas, who occasionally changed out of their normal clothing into mambo costumes with low, plunging backs and ruffled sleeves. On Saturday afternoon, he focused his attention on Juana the Mixe, who sat on a rock with her backside bared. When she felt him observing her, she turned, baring her teeth and a pair of white fangs. A few feet from her an older woman in petticoats and a woven sash sat spinning. Everything about the old woman looked dirty: her wrinkles, her clothing, her thighs, her toothless mouth.

"She's a virgin," Juana the Mixe revealed, "whore and everything. She got old figuring out how to not to give her hole to the clients."

A few steps away a teenager emerged from the river, bare breasted, hair soaking. She had been bathing, pouring water over her belly with a gourd.

The teen looked at Gabriel with greedy eyes. The gold of her skin looked burnished. A coral choker hung around her neck, and small earrings of the same material adorned her earlobes. On her breasts her nipples shone like purple flowers. A jug of water was balanced on her waist, her long fingers barely touching the clay. In her face Gabriel thought he saw a face from *The Book of Images*. But here she was in the present, irresistible as a vision given by the God Meat. He looked away from her and then, seconds later, their eyes would meet again.

"That's Conchita. You want to break her in?" asked El Popoluca.

"OK." Gabriel Jasón grabbed her hand and led her to the shack. Placing her on her knees, he then entered her from behind. He felt her bones creak as she doubled under his weight. Her eyes half-closed, she used her right hand to squeeze his balls and guided his fingers to her breasts. He pressed against her face so heavily it touched the floor. He kissed her back, her braids. He separated her cheeks, and with malice, trembling, joy, he entered her.

"Delicious girl, precious brown corn flower," said El Popoluca when he heard the sound of the door opening and saw Gabriel coming out of the shack. "I'll give you a good price for that jewel from Costa Chica.* I'd be selling you a jaguar, jaguar eyes, jaguar fangs, jaguar body, night all over, and filled with wind and fire."

"I couldn't pay for her."

"Think it over. Not even María Antonieta Pons had such beautiful thighs," insisted El Popoluca, while Conchita watched him out of the corner of her eye.

A little later a group of musicians from the highlands arrived on foot. They were dressed in white, and they carried wind instruments, a trombone, a trumpet, a saxophone. They wore straw sombreros and played music that the girls danced to with stiffened backs and monotonous, rhythmic stomping. All of the girls wanted to dance with Gabriel

*Costa Chica is an area along the coastline of the state of Guerrero with a large population of Afro-Mexicans, who are the descendants of enslaved African peoples.

Jasón, and they took their turns spinning around with him until he was left exhausted. The Tehuana, dressed up in an outfit of flounced lace and a skirt of embroidered flowers, her breast adorned with gold coins and chains, invited him to take a turn with her. Her face looked like a moon ringed in the lace of her white huipil, and he couldn't tell if her tiny mouth invited kisses or bites. Because Gabriel Jasón was sitting resting on the ground, she gave him her hand so he would get up and keep dancing with her.

The night before last I went to your house
Three whacks I gave to the padlock
You're no good to your lovers
You're in a deep sleep
¡Ay! Sandunga, Sandunga máma por Dios

In the evening a truck arrived carrying pigs, turkeys, packages of cigarettes, bottles of mezcal, and boxes of beer bottles. The visitors, along with El Popoluca, sat outside in the fresh air to eat tacos filled with fried grasshoppers, a posole of beans, chicken tamales, and sweet tamales.

"Stay here with us, compadre. You will have love and even your own daughter," said El Popoluca while the little girl watched Gabriel Jasón as if he was her future father.

"This is everything I have," Gabriel Jasón said, showing him his empty pockets.

"Fuck, then, how are you going to pay the bill? You're a real loser."

"I can't stay here. I'm going to wander the world."

"Come on, Rosa Quetzal's pimp, I'll loan you a .45 so you can take care of her. She's like a bird with red tits and green ass. She has a sweet peck and four-toed feet. She is *una* beauty with *dos* wings," said El Popoluca, who had been a farmhand in California and so spoke sometimes in Spanglish.

Gabriel Jasón sat thinking. All of a sudden, a strong storm blew in with the sound of thunder. Juana the Mixe ran up to tell El Popoluca that he should call the mayor of the town below to bring his keys and shut the lightning up in jail.

"Fuck," El Popoluca said, brandishing his machete blade at the lightning as if it meant to strike his women. He didn't relax until he saw a battle of flashes off over the hills of Huautla.

The musicians left in the rain, the storm passed, and the Tehuanas returned. Naked among the pines, with their feet green from stomping through the grass, their chests purpled, their muscles orange, and black haired with translucent braids, the group of women looked like a hallucination. But it was Rosa Quetzal, poised at the entrance or the exit of a cave, who most struck Gabriel Jasón as she was transforming into the most catlike woman he'd ever seen. There were circles painted like the spots of a jaguar all over her breasts, buttocks, and belly. Terrified, he saw her turn into an animal: the line of her nose spread, her cheeks hollowed out, her lips filled, her shoulders dropped, the skin of her ears and her temples splayed back, and under her brows nestled two oval eyes. Contorting her body in a great burst of concentration, an ancestral feline seemed to possess her; another head emerged from her head, and its slithering snout snapped at the air. So transformed, she led Gabriel Jasón to the shack, where she proceeded to throw him to the floor and cover him from head to toe with gashes and bites.

The Tehuanas drank chilled beers out of a cooler as twilight spread over Cerro de la Adoración. But they weren't interested in the twilight; what they were interested in was El Popoluca loosening his belt as he walked toward one of them. Suddenly Gabriel Jasón stopped. A girl appeared among the cacti chewing on coffee beans. Her body and face were smeared with green paint; she seemed irresistible. Exhausted by the screw with Rosa Quetzal, he closed his eyes as she walked by, clearly anxious to return to Huautla and his beatnik friends.

"Don't leave the party. Wait until dawn and leave with a full heart."

"I can't."

"Fuck," said El Popoluca and reluctantly loaned him a mule for his journey.

19

THE RETURN OF THE CHILEAN POET

A rain of golden light fell through the crack-filled roof of the market. It was afternoon, and the faces and bodies of the merchants were illuminated with an otherworldly splendor whose errant sparks slid over the walls and slithered along the corridors like celestial fire. White columns fell across the fruit and vegetable stands, the opened flesh of the animals hanging on hooks, and the kebabs all glistening in this explosion of life. Even the eyes of doña Anita smoldered like black fire. So extraordinary was the splendor of the moment that to Philip it seemed the light was alive.

"Look who's coming. The Chilean poet," said Barbara.

"From the way he's looking, he's going to make love to every female, hen, ewe, doe, or girl that he encounters," responded Philip. "He comes to the market on the pretext of eating mushroom tacos and drinking beer, but it's more like he comes to devour all the local girls with his eyes."

"I never imagined I would see you walking across Huautla in your underwear," Barbara said to Gabriel as he sat down with them in doña Anita's stall. "You fled under the cover of night. You ran so fast you left your shadow behind. A skinny silhouette, a fleeing silhouette, you ran away faster than your fear."

"Panic makes my feet winged." The Chilean poet grabbed a taco with grasshoppers and chewed it with delight. "I felt trapped, beaten to a pulp, carved up by those cruel men. My fear was that a wall would block my way, that I would fall into a well, that I would stumble upon a policeman who would sacrifice me. My big shoes smashed soft creatures underfoot: lizards, flies, and spiders squirmed on the ground in an omelet of legs and goop. I had had no sustenance, but I could have run until next year."

"How do you even seduce women that don't speak Spanish?" asked Philip.

"I recite Neruda verses, which they don't understand, and García Lorca verses, which they also don't understand, and I show them avocados, whose name in Nahuatl means 'testicles.'"

"Are you turned on by that?"

"I don't get hot for slack breasts or flat asses, but I do find sexiness in their modesty. In the dark their eyes glow like they have eaten ground obsidian. But most of all I love to praise their teeth. A woman who kisses and doesn't bite or drool isn't a woman. And I'm excited by the health of smooth, dazzlingly white teeth. They're erotic cornrows inside a closed mouth. The white teeth of Casimira and Delfina, for example, are a product of pre-Hispanic culture; remember, a maize plant grew out of the cracked head of an Olmec god-goddess like a personification of the earth offering her fertility. Zapotec gods carry tender kernels of corn deep in their ears. Among the Mixtec, maize was thought of as a symbol of womanhood, and among the Maya it was represented by a goddess with her pubis in the shape of maize between her thighs. I don't remember if the kernels were white, blue, red, yellow, or black, the colors of time and space, but I know that the colors inside of them are the color of extinguished fire. But I don't care if Casimira and Delfina's teeth are a product of mythological maize or criollo maize—their teeth shine when they smile. There are fetishists obsessed with shoes, hair, waists, earlobes. I'm obsessed with teeth."

"And what of Teonanácatl?"

"For some the God Meat is a hallucinogenic mushroom; for others, like me, the God Meat is the body of a woman."

"Tell us where you were," asked Barbara.

"Amigos, I owe you an explanation. Things happen. I was in the corral when Casimira appeared, swaying like a chick in heat. She might have an ugly head, but she has revealing curves. It rained. The violet, a flower praised for its modesty, is not very demure. The concubine of José Venancio passed by the hallway close to my room. I met her there. She lowered her eyes. There were barely contained curves. The line of her ass was visible; she looked at me sidelong. I focused on her feet. The door. I opened the door so she could come into my room. She came in. She got on her knees. I wanted her laid out. She raised up her skirt. She wasn't wearing anything underneath. It was like a tollbooth raising the arm so that a car could pass. I pounded her silently. With her sleepy eyes, she allowed it, she gave her consent, "Yes, young man." Fully aware that she was like the violet that doesn't open its chalice fully, I vanquished her. I opened a path through her eager filaments in the form of a mouth. She grabbed the sheets with her skinny fingers. She pretended to notice the wall. And in free fall, I let it happen, I penetrated her. She pretended to be docile in the act. Like an aquatic plant, the conjunction of the female sexual organs was finished and (in the form of carnivorous mouths in place of the masculine in the form of rods) the union of sperm was consummated. After a moment of repose, she got up. She fixed her hair in front of the mirror. She looked at me sidelong, not directly. Can you see it? Now that I think about it, I don't even know how the act was accomplished."

"And what happened with Delfina?"

"Delfina, with her dolphin name, is a playful body in the air and the water."

"And all the angry lovers?" Philip was distracted looking out of the window at two red-headed vultures perched on a branch. They had dragged a chicken with a slashed neck up into the tree with them.

"What are you looking at?" asked Gabriel Jasón. "Since when are those birds that look like Dominican friars at a public burning of a heretic more interesting than me?"

"I've counted fifty of them on light poles, highways, cliffs, and in the ravines since last week. This weekend that number will surely reach one hundred," explained Barbara.

"On Cerro Rabón there are rocky hollows and dead trees where they incubate and feed their hatchlings. They don't actually nest," Philip clarified. "What the swan is to Baudelaire's Parisian tableau, the vulture is to my Oaxacan painting."

"I need help," exclaimed Gabriel Jasón. "Hide me."

Barbara looked down her nose at him, as if her body was keeping her focused at a point on the ground. She paid little notice to his plight.

"How do you expect us to hide a man of your corpulence? Here come Howard and Guadalupe, ask them for help," said Philip, washing his hands of him.

"Howard, the flesh is sad, and I've read all the books. I find myself in a difficult situation. I am sleeping outdoors; I will die of pneumonia in this foreign land."

Howard shook his hand and scrutinized him with an affable face.

"What do you say?" Gabriel released his fingers. "Let me spend the night on a sleeping mat."

"Until when?" asked Guadalupe.

"Until yesterday, when José Venancio lessens his anger and lets me back into my room. Tomorrow I'll ask to cash some travelers' checks, and since his greed is stronger than his honor, he'll choose the money. Moreover, he prefers to sleep with the flag of the Republic of Spain over his concubines."

"Promise me that during the night you won't sleepwalk and climb into bed with me."

"I wouldn't dream of it. But I'll warn you that since I was a schoolboy I have been a con artist. I attended math class with my eyes focused in another direction, my physical eyes on the bodies of the women in the class and my mental eyes on the women of the street. When the teacher in my Marxist school lectured the students that they needed to think with their heads and not their members, I imagined a schoolyard with a crowd of women with their thighs open. 'What a precocious boy,' I heard my English teacher say, though I couldn't take my eyes off of her legs. 'He has spent the whole semester with blank eyes,' she said. 'All of his senses were focused on me.'"

"Chin up. We'll see you tonight," Guadalupe said and left.

"Where will I go in the meantime?"

"Go to the Cine Alameda," Howard recommended. "Remember: there NEVER was a woman like Rita Hayworth as Gilda."

20

THE SEARCH FOR BLISS

Howard and Guadalupe wandered everywhere looking for María Sabina. They went to the market and to church asking for the shaman of the sacred mushrooms. But there was something about those two longhairs that made the local people distrust them, and so they gave them false directions. Herbalists and healers pretended not to understand the slurred Spanish of "el gringo y la china." Alleging that they didn't know where Sabina lived or saying that they had never heard of her, they offered to hold mushroom ceremonies of their own at excessive prices. A wizard with long white hair and the face of a fox came up to them and said that that woman was unworthy of the sacred tradition.

Once outside of the possible residence of María Sabina, Howard and Guadalupe just stood in front of her shack, waiting to see her leave. Or they hid in the brushwood following the movements of that slight woman who went out with no shoes on, like a sparrow flying low over the ground. Carrying a machete, she pretended not to see them, though she watched them sidelong as she dedicated herself to her farming chores, crossing the cornfields and the coffee fields with kilos of corn or coffee in her rebozo. "Poor little gringos, desperate to come to one of my veladas," she said to herself.

At the hour of dusk, Philip and Barbara sat on stones near the shack to contemplate the Cerro de la Adoración and to watch the movements of an eagle flying over the town. Gabriel Jasón arrived carrying a brilliant blue rock-and-roll guitar with a thin neck and an encino wood fret and proceeded to smoke marijuana. All this happened while María Sabina watched the Holy Spirit's passage through the air as it invisibly crossed the mountain range. Like her Mazatec ancestors, she felt devotion to the spirits and supernatural beings, the masters of the caves, the hills, the springs, and the rivers, believing that the ancient deities could be seen in the clouds and the landscape.

Howard and Guadalupe stalked her; they photographed her from a distance; they followed the movement of the candles through the rooms of her shack; and they spied on her to see if she took off her clothes and if she was human, whether she slept with a huipil on. She knew the foreigners were there because of their colored clothing and because of their voices and noises, which announced their presence to her even in the dark.

Miss Pike and the teacher Herlinda had told her not to get involved with those stoners because they were troublemakers. Moreover, the poor ox they were using as a horse to spy on her with was at the point of collapse due to the weight of their bodies.

Richard Stevenson had charged the mycologists with chasing away the beatniks, arguing that Sabina already had enough problems, with her long days working in her corn and bean fields—she didn't have time to deal with them. The photographer threatened the trespassers with a call to the police if they continued to come on her property. But they refused to be intimidated, and while stepping playfully on the stones as if they were the stairs of the morning, only to return after a short while, they claimed they would wear down the path to Cerro del Fortín.

"You don't get to come in." Stevenson raised his hand to stop Philip and Barbara.

"We came for the velada."

"Not invited. Go back where you came from."

"We want to see her."

"Not my problem."

"Who are you to stop us?"

"My name doesn't matter. I'm part of a team of mycologists who are studying María."

"We're searching for bliss."

"Go register yourselves in town hall, there's no office for such processes here." Stevenson turned his back on them and, walking hurriedly, he lost them on the street in a cloud of mosquitos.

It didn't end there. The photographer inquired about them at the Hotel Grande—he knew they were Guadalupe and Howard and Gabriel Jasón. They had the faces of celibates, even though they were all in couples. He knew all of them went around in dirty clothes and sandals, even though they were richer than the locals. Together or alone, they ascended and descended Cerro del Fortín in search of María Sabina. On occasion they recited the verses of Ginsberg: "In the bleak flat night of Yucatan / where I come with my own mad mind to study / alien hieroglyphs of Eternity," even though the mountainous Huautla was the opposite of the Yucatan plains.

Stevenson concentrated on harassing Philip and Barbara, whom he saw as rebels fighting the status quo. He took notes on their appearance and behavior: "She looks at people with her back to them, turning her head back over her shoulder. Her hair the color of fire is like a curtain that opens to allow two brown eyes of rare beauty to emerge. Her pale face seems to whisper, 'This way, please.' The one called Philip has tried to approach María Sabina to ask her questions and take photos with her. But I've told the shaman that those ugly Americans are broke, untrustworthy, and that she should shut the door on them. The closest the couple has come to meeting her was one Sunday on the street at the market. They followed her along the main road, but they lost her in the brushwood because María slipped away like a bird. What they didn't notice was that while they followed her, the police were following them."

Together Philip and Barbara went to the market, and together they went into shops to buy cigarettes: Delicados, or Alas, or Tigres, or

Faros. They ordered half a kilo of coffee and beer, either Sol or Corona or the local brand, or whatever there was, which tasted like urine. In the stalls they bought *queso blanco,* or tortillas tlayudas, and orange juice spiked lightning style with the house aguardiente. Philip, with a notebook in hand, noted the names of the shops that sold mole negro, pan de burro, purified water, and huipiles and the public bathrooms where no one, not even the devil himself, came out dirty. The announcements stuck up on the lampposts on Red Cross drives for vaccination campaigns against measles and rabies also seemed to interest him, like the one about the big dance that would take place in the Benito Juárez public school on September 16. It didn't matter to them that people watched them embrace, give each other quick kisses, tangle themselves in caresses. Stevenson photographed them making love in the brushwood while the setting sun burned their bodies. He photographed Barbara from behind, her cloth belt falling over her right knee. And all the while María Sabina, sitting on a stone outside her shack, watched her like a put-out fire under the afternoon sun.

"Has that lady lost her mind?" Tatiana said upon seeing Barbara naked and covering herself from the rain with a tiny umbrella. "I hope the policemen don't see her—they'll attack her."

"Tricked by the illusions of Tezcatlipoca, she's decided to lose herself in the forests of unreality." Gordon, sitting next to her, surprised her with his high-pitched laugh. "The queen of the underworld of our time is an Italian American Persephone. The couple reminds me of an epitaph of Luis de Góngora that I learned in my student days at Princeton. It goes more or less like this:

Love is like two eggs
Cracking open their well-being.
He is dropped into the water
And she is splayed out on a plate."

21

MISS EUNICE VICTORIA PIKE

"Day after day the greenness comes closer, fogging my vision. Like an avalanche, it sweeps over kilometers of meadows that look like fertile emeralds," Tatiana said as she ascended the street running directly into Cerro del Fortín.

"In the middle of the splendid agony of nature is our present. Like the time of the hills, it seems ancient and from the past," said Roger Hofmann in the company of his woman and child as he headed toward a velada with María Sabina.

"Is there a mirror in this shack?" asked Ivanna upon entering.

"No," replied Apolonia.

"Why not?"

"According to my mother, a person in a trance shouldn't see their own face. They could confuse their own expression with that of an evil person, and upon seeing their eye holes they might fall into the abyss of their selves."

"Miss Eunice Victoria Pike has made an appearance," announced the teacher Herlinda after the mycologists had settled themselves on seats and mats and María Sabina had greeted them with her hands.

"I bring a letter addressed to you." The evangelist, Eunice Victoria Pike, turned to Gordon.

"What is it regarding?"

"Instructions to understand the nature of the mushrooms. I wrote it March 9, 1953, so as to be meticulous. It's about the mushroom *si*[3] *tho*[3], known as *nti si*[3] *tho*[3]."

Herlinda interjected to introduce her: "Miss Pike is a Protestant missionary of impeccable conduct. Because of her long stay in Huautla, she knows the Mazatec language very well."

"The knowledge of the power of the mushroom is very long," Miss Pike read from her letter:

> The Mazatecs call it the Blood of Christ because they believe that it sprung up wherever drops of blood fell. They also claim that the mushroom helps those who are pure, more than someone unpure, whom they can kill or drive mad. When the people speak of "impurity" they refer to "ritual impurity": someone who has not abstained five days before or five days after from having sexual relations.
>
> The sorcerer eats the mushroom at night because he prefers to act without sight. Until nine o'clock he ingests and then begins to speak half an hour to an hour later. The Mazatecs speak of the mushroom as if it was a person. They never say, "The sorcerer said"; rather, "The mushroom said," directly quoting the mushroom.
>
> The healer eats four or five mushrooms raw. If they eat too many, the mushroom will try to kill them. If this situation arises, the sorcerer will fade and only recover his senses little by little, but his assistants will have to intercede on his behalf. These types of accidents can happen to any man or woman who has had sexual relations too soon before the ingestion of the Holy Children.
>
> If everything goes well, the sorcerer will have visions, and the mushroom will speak through him for a duration of two or three hours. It's Jesus Christ himself who speaks to us. The mushroom reveals what has happened to a sick person, and the sorcerer will be able to say if he was cursed and by whom and why. Or if he's sick with fear. Or if it is related to a sickness curable with medication, the sorcerer will suggest that they call a medic.

> For those who follow the rite, proof that Jesus Christ is speaking to them is in the visions experienced by whoever consumes this mushroom. Those we've interviewed said that they saw the sky itself. They insinuate, in different words, that they've seen a film in color. The majority say that the witches often see the sea, and for these mountain people, to see the sea is the pinnacle.

"I have asked about the appearance the sorcerer has under the influence of the mushroom," Miss Pike continued, reading from her letter. "They've told me that they don't sleep, that they are seated with eyes open, 'awoken.' In those moments they should not drink alcohol, although they can the following day. The next day, some sorcerers return to their work, but others stay at home to sleep, as they've tripped all night long."

Miss Pike continued: "I want to specify clearly that I lament the continuation of the use of the mushroom, because I know of no cases where it has been beneficial. I would prefer it if my Mazatec brothers would consult the Bible when they wanted to understand the designs of Christ and not be tricked by a sorcerer and his mushrooms.

"This is the end of this missionary's account. Please permit me to tell those who persist in their erroneous ways that the mushrooms appear two times a year, at the start and end of the rains. Thank you for your time," concluded Miss Pike, and, wrapped in shadow, she left the house.

The teacher Herlinda followed her, although she returned a few minutes later, to the surprise of those present, excepting those who were asleep, who didn't pay attention to either her presence or her absence.

"The austere Miss Pike was absent during the first part of our time in Huautla. She came during the second part, when my wife and I had the pleasure of meeting her," revealed Roger.

"There is a beatnik thrashing around out here. He says to call him Howard. He's with a Chinese woman named Guadalupe, and they asked about María Sabina," announced Stevenson. "If anyone knows them, great. If not, I need a hand in chasing them off."

Curious, the mycologists went outside. There was Howard, exhausted by his ascension of Cerro del Fortín, wearing a yellow sweatshirt and unwashed pants. He was carrying a sign:

RENT A BEATNIK

To make adobes
Roof a shack
To sow yellow marijuana
To care for chickens or roast pigs
To accompany your girlfriend to the market
To dance the jarabe "Flor de Naranjo"
To play hide-and-seek with your daughter in the cavern of Cerro Rabón
To wander around on Cerro de la Adoración
In exchange for room and board
By the day or the week
Rent a beatnik.

22

TRISTESSA

"Tristessa," exclaimed Jack Kerouac upon passing the decrepit building whose sordid roof terrace he had once shared with Esperanza Villanueva when he was living in Distrito Federal. The years 1955 and 1956 seem very long ago, but they kept returning to assault him in his dreams, the way Saint Augustine says that memory remembers even the forgotten.

"The last time I saw her, she was standing outside my door under the rain, right here, at like four in the morning. 'Jack, open up,' she said. But I didn't open for her. I pretended to be asleep. I was tired of the fact that every dawn she would come to lie with me in the greasy bed that barely had room for my body. The addicts that lived in the other servant quarters on the roof between gas tanks, laundry lines, and pots with dried-out geraniums had trudged off to the shacks in Garibaldi to sell themselves. 'Life is worth nothing. Life is worth nothing,' the mariachis sang in the ghostly streets of the Centro Histórico, where in ancient times the Aztecs removed hearts in dawn ceremonies.

"'Jack, open up.' After five minutes she had returned to beg me from the other side of the door. She was totally drenched, completely soaked, but I remained deaf to her pleas. Half an hour later, sitting on the ground, she started begging again, with no answer from me. And it wasn't until I didn't hear her voice or her ragged breathing anymore that I got up and opened the door. She wasn't there. From the terrace I leaned out over the stairs to look for her. I went out into the street in the downpour. I didn't find her in the alleys of the broken-down whorehouses on calle Violeta or calle 2 de Abril. I walked the neighborhood of Santa María la Redonda. I went into the Kiosco Morisco, built for the New Orleans World's Fair as the Mexican Pavilion; its lighted crown illuminated the humid dawn. I rummaged around the benches of the Alameda de Santa María. I went back to lie down. I felt miserable because I hadn't opened the door for her to get out of the rain." This memory was recorded by Gabriel Jasón between gulps of aguardiente on the yellow couch of the reception of Hotel Grande as he sat watching huge raindrops slipping down the thick glass panes of the windows.

"Tristessa." Gabriel Jasón remembered Jack Kerouac bursting out with her name while walking on a footbridge over a ditch of cars rushing through the netherworld of that polluted city. He remembered that the Beat poet lit another marijuana cigarette with the ember of the butt he was smoking. And he saw him clearly leaning on the handrail stripped and corroded by the acid air, looking below as if the river of cars passing were crushing the ghost of Esperanza Villanueva, the young Mexican morphine addict who had shared his drugs and his squalor between the filthy walls of that dump on that filthy rooftop. He stood there looking with eyes deep as chasms at the traffic passing over his shadow like the hide of a flattened dog. "It was on this bridge one night she suggested we should make a lesbian sex movie about La Muerte and Lady Nothing," Jack said. "I can still see her on the edge of the bed, listless, spread-eagle. Her nylon stockings torn. Her flowered skirt tossed on the floor. Her black sunglasses half on. A piece of cotton soaked in alcohol in her mouth. A print of the Virgin of Guadalupe watching her from the wall with enormous sadness in her face. 'Mehico. Oaksaka,' she would repeat. Drug addiction, you know."

"Tristessa," Allen Ginsberg said, "is a narrative meditation studying a hen, a rooster, a dove, a cat, a Chihuahua dog, family meat, and a ravishing, ravished junkie lady, first in their crowded bedroom, then out to drunken streets, taco stands, and pads at dawn in Mexico City slums."

"Tris-te-ssa," Gabriel Jasón believed Jack Kerouac yelled out that night in Huautla, while imagining them both in the Hospice of Vultures in that cannibal city. "We wandered the foul streets of the Vizcaínas, the Ring of Desolation, and the park of Masoch Sullivan, where the prostitutes hang out. We walked the trolley tracks that are no longer used; we were troubled by the bleary eyes at the entrances to the various neighborhoods. We sat on the park benches full of splinters that get lodged in the fat asses of the office bosses and in the pear-shaped butts of their secretaries. We wanted to eat some tacos but then saw the butcher kicking a grimy feral cat, and that act of unwarranted aggression against an animal made us furious, so we left, trampling over sleeping vagrants in store doorways wrapped in newspapers from days before. We got into a taxi for three pesos—with a tip, three and a half—and drove to the Ángel de la Independencia wrapped in smog. 'The Aztec needle pierces the flesh of the abandoned like a flame,' she said. 'The drug takes possession of your body and follows you like a demon everywhere, until it kills you. Help me to leave the nightmare of Mexico-Tenochtitlán-Distrito-Federal-where-Es-pe-ran-za-Vi-lla-nue-va-rests-in-the-chasm-of herself.' 'In the last earthquake the earth opened, but I didn't swallow you so that you would keep on swallowing yourself,' I told her," said Kerouac. "That night I was napping, was the last time I saw her, drunk from anguish in a rundown hotel on calle de Pino, in the neighborhood of Santa María la Redonda. All the time stepping on my shadow to sell drugs to an Indian with the eyes of a cockroach," said Gabriel Jasón/Jack Kerouac.

23

THE TRAVELING SALESMAN

"On almost the incendiary eve / Of several near deaths, / When one at the great least of your best loved / And always known must leave / Lions and fires of his flying breath. . . . In many married London's estranging grief." Gabriel Jasón read Ivanna the Dylan Thomas poem in the hotel restaurant, which had no other patrons at that time of night. Forty-watt bulbs gave the place a depressing air. The two alternated drinking swigs of coffee and swigs of aguardiente.

"Why did you come to Huautla?" she asked him.

"The God Meat." The waiter brought them the check, which Gabriel signed with a scrawl.

"What were you doing before?"

"I was living on office time, languishing in a nine-to-eight schedule. One morning, while looking at my face in the mirror, I opened my mouth to discover a huge lump under my tongue. Terrified by the possibility that it was cancer, I quickly left and ran out to the street, filled with an anxiety to live before the illness consumed me. I abandoned my tyrannical woman, I didn't return to the office, and I declared myself a free agent. I decided that I would never again clock in on a gray machine, I slipped off my name tag at the end of a line of submissive employees in front of a boss with hair coming out of his ears and women who put on their makeup in the bathroom before sitting down at their desks on asses like slowly spreading cushions. I escaped the jail of my days, and I became a holy fool," declared Gabriel Jasón. "I traveled from country to country with no papers identifying me as a man employed by who knows who. My only possession was myself, though I also carried a little money in my pocket. My passport was stolen on a bus by some idiot who didn't even know how to read."

"Can I bring you anything else?" The waiter had returned.

"A beer."

"Would you like to store your suitcase? We have a room for luggage. We don't give a receipt, just note your name with chalk."

"I have no suitcases. When you want to throw me in the street, do it. I'm used to moving around and sleeping wherever I happen to pass the night."

"Don't rush off, you can always pay your lodging to don Venancio with your body."

Just then a cadaverous man dressed in gray appeared in the hotel, a cigarette held between his trembling fingers. He looked so tense that he gave the impression he couldn't stand up by himself. Waiting in reception, he fell into such a long silence that the hotelier impatiently and repeatedly asked how he could be of assistance.

"Name?"

"Juan Rulfo. Traveling salesman for Goodrich-Euzkadi. I am visiting in order to sell used tires to local footwear businesses for huaraches."

"The reason for your visit isn't important. Do you want a room?"

"A standard room. One night. Away from the mariachis and parades. I'll be departing at dawn with the first bus. If not sooner." The visitor lit a new cigarette with the butt of the old one and then stamped out the smoking one.

"You look tired."

"From listening to coyotes howl in the mountains all night. In the bus there was a woman coming from Toluca who said her husband was thrown into the sea on a life preserver of sausages and drowned. She didn't stop complaining the whole time she was sitting next to me—that the windowpanes were dirty, that one of the passers was snoring a lot, that the boy behind us smelled bad, that I looked very green, and so on."

"Place of birth?"

"Comala, a ghost town."

"The inhabitants left?"

"The bogeyman swallowed them up."

"So it's quiet."

"You don't hear bodies with no feet stirring at night."

"Are you traveling with anyone?"

"No. The woman on the bus reminded me of a Costa Rican poet named Eunice Odio, enemy until death of the tenth muse, the Mexican Pita Amor, but when we arrived in Huautla she fled. I remember that Eunice Odio lived on calle Río Nazas, and the señoras couldn't stand her because she liked to show off her panther-like curves on the patio of her building. Indeed, it was a habit of hers to sunbathe or moon bathe naked, which inspired the ire of her neighbors, including that of my wife, because all the husbands and sons leaned out of the windows of their bedrooms to watch her or peeked out at her from the cracks of their open doors in the hallways of the first floor. She wore her sunglasses and pretended not to notice the excitement she caused."

"Did you spy on her too?"

"I preferred to hide in the café of the pediatric hospital, near my house. No one went to that café, except the relatives of the children who were being treated for illness or accident. The only bother there was that near the candy store was a public pay phone and the parents used it to speak with their relatives, at times whimpering over the lamentable state of their offspring. For me those blasts of reality were inspiration to finish my next book, which I hadn't yet started."

"Does the woman on my wall turn you on?"

"What woman?"

"That one." José Venancio pointed at Cyd Charisse on the wall.

"The photo?"

"Doesn't she look majestic?"

"It's been some time since I passed the age of getting excited over photos in magazines. One day my mother found me in the bathroom thinking, just thinking . . ."

"You can tell me later. Now up to your room." The hotelier signaled to Casimira, who helped him with his luggage, which was covered in ad stickers for tire companies.

"They say that there's a woman around here who cures people with hallucinogenic mushrooms. I cure myself by sleeping."

"So you won't be attending one of her veladas."

"My insomnia ceremonies are enough for me."

"Not even for your nerves?"

"For my nerves, I drink my mezcal."

"Casimira, take the gentleman to his room."

"I'll take a nap before breakfast." The guest wouldn't allow Casimira to carry his luggage. He closed the door to the room, and after a long nap he woke in the middle of the night.

"Where am I? What time is it? Why are there no clocks on the walls?" asked the guest in the darkness. Later he went out into the corridor and down to the restaurant, where Philip was drinking coffee and smoking marijuana.

"Do you work here?" Rulfo asked, turning all his attention on him.

"No."

"What do you take for the cold in these puny excuses for mountains?"

"The moonlight peeking out from behind that peak."

"That seems about right."

"And you?"

"The screeching of the cicadas keeps me from sleeping, that's why I got up. When I turned on the light, I saw the insects were on the pillow. Their company was short-lived, very much so, because I left them nesting on my socks and smashed them with a shoe."

"How considerate."

"The hallway was even worse. On the way to the bathroom, I trampled the hands and feet of the twenty-four sons of General Zamudio whom he had with his seven concubines. He brought them here to initiate them in the cult of the hallucinogenic mushroom so that they would return home as worthy men. They were laid out on the floor on mats with their bodies splayed in sleep. Not only did they not let me pass, but they also wanted to beat me up. Because there weren't enough rooms for them, the hotelier had installed them on the floor of the hallway outside my room. The worst of all of them was the general, though. He was so suspicious I had wanted to assault his daughter with his fifth concubine (he has only one daughter, one mare, and twenty-three stallions) that he started to shoot into the air to alert his progeny. Not only that, when I was finally in front of the toilet starting to piss, I aimed wrong, and a yellow stream of liquid spilled on his most beloved child, and he almost killed me. He started to insult me and chased after me, so I ran to hide out here, with you. I've noticed they have no idea what service is in this establishment fit for donkeys, there's no one to serve you a cup of hot coffee." Juan Rulfo stood up from the table smoking a cigarette.

"You're leaving without even a snack?"

"I'm going to go out and walk around to see the town at night."

"I'll go with you."

"Wait for me a moment. I'm going to fetch my sample case. I'll leave directly for the bus terminal."

"I'll wait for you."

"I have a meeting at nine in the morning to sell tires to a huarache maker; it will save me from making another trip again in the year 2000. It's cold as a thousand fucks, let's go, it's starting to look a lot like Comala." Rulfo lit another cigarette, and he and Philip went out into the main street, desolate in the dawn. They stopped in front of a hall in ruins that was called the Cinema Alameda, next door to the Gran Tienda, whose entryway was a narrow door between two display windows illuminated with light bulbs. On the peeling wall a poster announced *La Furia del Caribe*, the last movie of the rumba queen María Antonieta Pons.

"The Mazatecs, lovers of trances and psychedelic trips, aren't really affected by horror movies and swaying hips. The screening of *The Bride of Frankenstein* was a complete flop." Rulfo pointed at an old poster of Elsa Lanchester. The actress had crazed eyes and a mouth like a black flower, her hair stood up in an electrified perm, and she seemed to be just leaving the laboratory and the resurrection. Rulfo shrugged his shoulders, touched the closed-down doorway, and with a movement of his head signaled toward two tottering shadows leaning against a wall. Philip could just make out Gerhart. Standing outside the bar the Staggering Monkeys, which was closed at this hour, Gerhart held a bottle of aguardiente in his hand. A little further off Vera Lawson, his muse, stumbled, inebriated. Ghosts of themselves, they didn't recognize him.

A man completely surrounded by women appeared suddenly. From Gabriel Jasón's descriptions, Philip recognized Popoluca, Rosa Quetzal, Tomasa the Tehuana, Juana the Mixe, and Teresa the Tzeltal with her almond-eyed daughter. The tight-mouthed pimp with high cheekbones had come down from the hills in his white pants, patent leather shoes, and colored vest to open a club in town he would call Mambo No. 5.

Suddenly Juan Rulfo, his suitcase in hand, began to walk away from the theater without saying goodbye to Philip. He seemed more interested in catching the first bus of the day than in taking a walk down memory lane, talking about horror in the cinema, or returning to bed. The poet from San Francisco, standing next to the clock tower, watched him go as he passed in front of the houses near the market, and then he lost sight of him in the depths of the night. He disappeared on the way to the bus station like a vertical, weightless, and distant shadow.

24

VISIONS

María Sabina wasn't home. Philip found the door open and sat down to wait for her. In the room where the veladas were held, he examined the saints that were positioned on top of the table. It still smelled of copal from the velada held on Thursday, and there on a tray were the landslide mushrooms.

"Who's there?" María Sabina asked in Mazatec. Her brown face tightened by the sun, she looked fragile but strong. Her black braids fell down her front over her huipil. As if she knew he was there before she saw him, she nodded toward him in the darkness.

"I've come to meet you," said Philip.

"My mother says there are other healers in town," Apolonia translated her words for him. "What happened to you?"

"I fell climbing Cerro del Fortín, that's why I am using a walking stick. I don't want a ceremony with another healer, all I want is her. The idea of trying mushrooms in one of her veladas has become an obsession to me. I've tried drugs in San Francisco, but instead of bringing me closer to God, they distanced me from him. I dream of trying the Holy Children, given to me from her hands and which she has sanctified with her copal."

"My mother says she understands, but she's very busy. In Huautla there are many sick people; with the mushrooms she needs to diagnose their infirmities and heal them in her veladas with songs and litanies."

"Tell her I understand, but for me it is of utmost importance to pierce the threshold of the visions."

"She says, 'To cross the vision threshold isn't so simple.'"

"Tell her that to come here with my partner has been difficult, but now that we are here we cannot return to the US without attending a velada with her. It doesn't matter how much she charges us. We will give her everything that we can give."

"Don't try to negotiate with the spirit. She doesn't charge for the veladas; she only receives what the people willingly give her."

"We can give her all the money we have."

"'It's not a matter of money,' she says."

"Señora, I want you to show me how to see the world as it is inside and out. I want you to show me how to see life." She listened to him without raising her head but still registering what he said.

"María Sabina says that every person sees the world in their own way. The world that one sees is not the same as the world that another sees, and looking at the same thing, everyone sees differences. In that way, one thing seems to us two things: that which one person sees and that which the other sees. The vision of one thing changes as the hours pass, along with the state of the spirit, without ever moving location. What changes is us. While we look at something it can change inside of us, and in that way, it can also change the state of our spirit."

"The sacred mushrooms can help one have a clearer vision of things?"

"One should learn to look at the world with their own eyes, helped by the eyes of others, yes, but when one learns to walk alone they should throw away the crutches."

"Do you think there is any chance that the señora would accompany me on my journey?"

"María Sabina does not say yes or no."

"I don't want to spend my time in Huautla cheered up by a little mezcal or a marijuana joint," Philip yelled. "I want to know María Sabina."

"I understand, but she says no-yes."

"I can obtain the mushrooms for the velada."

"Only she knows which ones; only she knows how to give them in pairs of male and female." Apolonia removed her rebozo.

"When will you give me a date to visit?" Philip asked exasperatedly. "This is why I came to Huautla, to see the señora."

María Sabina rose from her seat. She looked at him, lit a thick cigar, and sat back down.

"My mother wants to know if you've visited other witches in the town and who they were."

"None, I just came to see her."

"Have you bought plants from the herbalists?"

"Some medicinal ones."

"My mother wants to know if you've tried the peyote."

"I've never hung out with the Huichol."

"My mother wants to know how long you will be here."

"That depends on her."

"Where are you staying?"

"At the Hotel Grande."

"My mother asks how you knew how to find her."

"From José Venancio, the hotelier."

"Apart from wandering around, what is your profession?"

"I write poetry."

"She asks if you have a girlfriend."

"One. She came with me."

"Just one."

"Yes."

"Have you visited the Cerro de la Adoración?"

"Yes."

"Did you like it?"

"Yes."

"She says that in one part of the hill there is a cave where a white jaguar lives, her nagual."

"Is it dangerous?"

"To some people."

"I like white jaguars, and black ones, and spotted ones." Upon hearing him María Sabina opened her eyes, which had been halfway closed.

"My mother asks if you've eaten."

"No."

"My mother makes a good black mole. She invites you to eat with her."

"What can I do in order for her to hold a velada for me?"

"Eat these mushrooms."

Philip ate them.

"Close your eyes, concentrate on nothing."

After a while, with his legs crossed, in a daze, Philip saw a figure walking toward him outside of the shack; the figure's eyes were looking fixedly toward the Cerro de la Adoración. It was her twin. He and the figure started to advance toward each other. On the way, the double stopped. On Cerro del Fortín, he saw Dolores walking up. He doubted that the sorceress was real. Even when she entered the shack and he saw her undress, he couldn't believe it. The sorceress sprayed her armpits, butt, breasts, and pubic area with perfume. From her chin she hung a tuft of horsehair like a beard. She pointed the spray toward the mirror and perfumed the reflection of Philip. Later Dolores entered the room where María Sabina was conducting the velada with the Holy Children, and in a bizarre trance she parodied María's dancing and movements with obscene gestures. When she attempted to read *The Book of Images*, she found the pages empty. Twisting in her arms were two vipers flickering obscene tongues from between their jaws. When the bells of San Juan Evangelista rang out, Dolores vanished.

"Who is that person with the Sicilian American face?" Stevenson asked Apolonia a few feet away from Philip.

"That's me. His name is Philip, and he's thirty years old," the aforementioned introduced himself. "He lives in the Hotel Grande. His goal in life is to become a great poet. For that reason, he came to this town to meet the mushroom priestess."

"He has a face like he spends a lot of time looking in the mirror."

"He does that to see if the boy he was hasn't been disfigured by the years."

"I owe him an apology."

"Why?"

"I riled up the antagonism of my group against you. I photographed him-you in secret. I understand now that the beatniks are more dangerous to themselves than others, and sometimes the people surrounding them are more evil than they are."

"I *know*."

"He can stay at the velada."

"Thank you, but I didn't know you were the priestess's mayordomo."

Gordon, who was also present, leaned over to Philip: "I'd like to confide my reflections: We can see our life in images, we can inhabit the camera of the mind in seconds. Past, present, and future coexist in our interior film. The only thing that ends is the action of the projector of memory, so that our existential faces detonate and our memories are revealed in real time. Amnesia and dreams, visions and hallucinations interweave and unravel, occur and are challenged outside of our control, at their own velocity. For a few moments we believe that we have access to the panorama of our existence, but it all seems to be a flight of imagination."

"That's a nice thought," murmured Philip.

Roger Hofmann revealed, "Like in the book *Misérable miracle* by Henri Michaux: 'Himalayas all at once spring up higher than the highest mountain, sharply pointed, but false peaks, diagrams of mountains, though not less high for all that, inordinate triangles with angles ever more acute, to the very edge of space, idiotic but immense.'"

"Interesting," responded Philip.

Stevenson confessed: "It's impossible to take photos of the visions caused by mushrooms. I am stuck with exteriors, with superficialities; what is seen, what is heard by the participants, escapes me. The images that they perceive and the voices they hear are interior; they occur in a time outside of time. Even though the zoom lens draws close, their insides are incomprehensible, they remain distant. I am left with what is captured by the roll in the film canister."

From out of the gloom, Hofmann exploded: "Michaux in *Misérable miracle* had a vision in white. He said: 'Absolute white. White whiter than all whiteness. White of the advent of white. White without compromise, by exclusion, by the total eradication of non-white. White, mad, exasperated, shrieking with whiteness. Fanatical, furious, riddling the eyeball. White, atrociously electric, implacable, murderous. White in blasts of white. God of "white." No, not a god, a howler monkey.'"

"Every one has their vision. Every ego their own sleeping mat. Every one with their particular tone of voice," mused Philip, watching Howard and Gabriel as they kept up an animated exchange about their experiences with the mushrooms. The former argued with himself, and the latter searched out the attention of his neighbor on the floor. The women Barbara, Guadalupe, Ivanna, and Tatiana passed in front of everyone with their eyes closed, with their eyes open on an imagined catwalk of black space. Like people lost on familiar streets, like characters in an interior movie, or like dolls on a shelf in an antique store, with tags hanging from their neck with the price of sale, the four represented both a real moment and a moment passed. They provoked a tiredness in Philip with their ceaseless coming and going, an emptiness that was filled and abandoned by their walking. Their bodies in movement, their dramatic clothes (which in reality they weren't wearing), and their high heels (which they weren't wearing) represented them as being larger than themselves, part of an outwardly intimate spectacle. They didn't look like themselves. "How I want to paint them and write them on the canvas of intangibility. Describe them with colors like in a self-portrait. The ego daydreaming becomes another. And to see them up close is like being in a trance," said Philip.

Gabriel Jasón said to Howard: "It makes me happy to see you where I don't expect you, in the magic comfort of this site of veneration and of ill repute. From what I can see, death dignifies your smile."

"Jasón, don't be so lazy," chastised Guadalupe.

Philip left them. In his vision he imagined his double sleeping on a mat with legs extended, just like him. The upper part of his head touched the floor, just like his. His lookalike regarded him without sympathy, as if he was a stranger he was uninterested in knowing. He had the sensation that the individual who looked like him sprang from another Philip. They both looked at a plate that was being circulated. Both Philips ate the fruit on it with their eyes. Both tilted their ears so as to watch them breathe. Until at last the fruit jumped onto the table and the plate remained behind, abandoned. Philip smiled. In a chair was a mandarin offering itself to his hands. His double began to peel it. Its sections trembled as if it was feeling pain. The other Philip let it drop. The fruit peered up at him from the floor through its peel. The other Philip kneeled down before it and picked it up. Like an open mouth the plate closed around it and recovered it. Philip watched himself walking toward San Francisco. He felt the rain in his finger leaves and heard the drops slide down his trunk. He woke in the city. But he wasn't there. Like a Mohave he witnessed the feverish rain of 1848 at the beginning of the gold rush. Terrestrial shifting shook its neighborhoods, while he and Barbara surrendered to making love in the bay. Their naked bodies assumed the form of mushrooms that refused to be uprooted from the sky while the sun burned their bodies. Fixed there they gave the impression of holding lightning in their hands and in their darkened feet. Their interlaced bodies were nightened by the dawn. Philip unfolded himself. He saw himself in the body of Howard making love to Guadalupe, being urinated on by a dog. A fog surrounded the bed made of brushwood. Vultures with red heads pecked their buttocks. The voices of the plants slipped from green to green, through the mountain, through the water, through the breasts of Guadalupe. She heard them in her body as if they were her own voice. They didn't speak to her, they spoke to themselves. Then Philip felt himself leave in the body of someone else who was named Philip, change into the living color of self-aware vegetation. He saw his body leave, cross the here and now and the distance to Cerro de la Adoración.

"What's wrong, señora?" he heard Apolonia ask Barbara, disturbed by the vision expressed by her face. In a corner of darkness, she was barely visible, sitting on a wool rug.

"I just had the nightmare of the serpent, the one where the viper climbs up your legs without biting you," she said.

"Where were you, señora? I mean, were you the serpent?"

"I was mounted on a white horse. All of a sudden, a cloud came down full of moving points. Millions of lice overran the bushes, the brush, the countryside. The shade that projected over the ground sank into shifting sands that had not been there before. The lice jumped over one another. The green of the grass, the yellow of the flowers, the moss of the stones were all covered with those insects with their flat, wingless bodies. There were so many it made me want to cut my hair so they wouldn't nest in my hairy hide. Thousands of them attacked the head of a blind man—they were hanging behind his earlobes, they penetrated his nostrils and mouth, fell into his eyes. Before their advance all space was narrowed, all bodies were insufficient."

"What else did you see, Barbara?" said Philip, trying to fight off his drowsiness.

"The lice emerged from the stomach of an old horse, from plastic bags, broken bottles, from clothes, and shoes, and pillows. They didn't spare the leaves or the flowers or necks or pubic areas. In the beds of lovers, they nested in genitals. The swarm came from Central America and entered Mexico by its southern border, and from there it spread toward the United States. In Huautla the alarm was sounded among the silkworm farmers, but the mulberry leaves were infested by the lice and no longer served to feed the silkworms, and then the trees died."

"Wow." Stevenson coughed.

"With my nails I popped lice like chestnuts in the fire. Their hairy hides burst in crowns of red, white, black, and yellow," continued Barbara.

"I dreamed that a legion of giant cockroaches made an assault on New York," said Ivanna.

"I saw the heads of old men infested with lice, as if their bad thoughts had escaped to their exteriors. They needed tweezers to pull them out from the roots of their hair. Male and female lice ranging from yellow to black to white to gray to chestnut rose up my thighs," continued Barbara.

"Continue."

"The lice jumped out from the seams and folds of clothing and bathing suits and from armpits and groins and eyelashes and eyebrows of the whores of New York/Babylonia. In a swarm they wandered all over the lush lower bellies of whores to lay their eggs during sex."

"Anything else?"

"Millions of fleas penetrated bodies and procreated in the streets. They slid off the seats of toilet bowls and swam to their little deaths in the black water. A bodiless voice advised me to follow the advice of Doctor Tango. It was the voice of the Comte de Lautréamont: 'If the land is covered with lice, as many as grains of sand in the sea, the human race will be annihilated, victims of their terrible desires.'"

"Are you sure he said *ardores*, desires?

"I don't know, I'm just telling you I feel uneasy in my heart."

"When are you going to give me the opportunity to attend a velada?" Philip asked María Sabina.

"You just did," the shaman responded.

25

CRUNCHY CANNIBAL COITUS

When Philip and Barbara were returning from the market along a steep street, they glimpsed a black iguana moving in the brushwood, camouflaged by the vegetation. Its skin was covered with small scales that looked like scabs and was so wrinkled and parched, it was basically a shell. From the dorsal crest to its armpit, the *Ctenosaura pectinata* looked like a slimy rock, as if it was living in an ancient present. When it saw Philip, it bared its teeth and tried to slink off, but it stumbled and was trapped against a wall. The cacti in the evening looked backlit, etched out by seams of light.

"In reality it's not an iguana. It doesn't have the jowls, the blinking eyelids, or four limbs. It's a person. And moreover, a person who shares a last name with a typewriter."

"It's William Burroughs!" exclaimed Philip. "What's he doing wandering through Huautla?"

"The last time I saw his photograph it was in a Mexican newspaper. In a Superman outfit, with his customary fedora, he had just finished smashing a television set in the lobby of the hotel he was staying at, telling the receptionist, 'I despise Benito Juárez.'"

"He came to Mexico to live on calle Cerrada de Medellín to evade charges of drug possession in New Orleans. While observing the Mexican sky, Burroughs wrote: 'That special shade of blue that goes so well with circling vultures, blood, and sand—that raw menacing pitiless Mexican blue.'"

"He killed his wife playing at William Tell, right?" asked Barbara.

"At number 122 on calle Monterrey during a wild party he placed a glass on her head and shot at it with a .38 Star automatic, shooting her in the forehead. His lawyer, the wife killer Bernabé Jurado, moved to have the crime declared an accident. In the end, corruption does have its advantages: the crime was declared an accident by the authorities. 'Freed,' bragged Bill."

"Did you visit him when he lived in the Colonia Roma?"

"I ran into him once sitting on a bench on Plaza Río de Janeiro, bare breasted, airing his wrinkled nipples. His eyes were glazed over, and he was talking to himself. Under the effects of heroin, he would sometimes pass several hours staring at his big toe. Or he would leave his den to hunt little boys," stated Philip.

"Like a lizard stalking hares in the brushwood."

"'Cheap Mexican boys, worth three pesos,' Bill boasted. 'Better if they are from the poor areas—they're more willing to sell themselves in public restrooms. Three pesos each, beggars, porters, schoolboys, shoeshine boys, street kids hoping for clients in the Indianilla tram station, outside of a hotel, or leaning against a wall. Grubby, shoeless, skin dirty from sleeping on the ground or on iron benches, baring their skinny flesh and tight asses through their rags. You have to wash them before fucking them,' he always said, deep under the influence of tequila and drugs. In the company of his lawyer, Bernabé Jurado, he visited the brothels of La Bandida, where politicians, police chiefs, and drug dealers would kill the waiters and prostitutes for fun to the tune of 'La Cucaracha.' That man walked through moral and physical ruins, he passed his days sprawled on the floor injecting himself with heroin, then he went out to the streets to find boys. He carried a .45 and fifty-peso bullets to use against the police."

As Philip recounted this, William stood up in the scrub brush. For the first time in her life, Barbara saw an iguana stand up and button his jacket. Wearing a pistol at his hip and a felt fedora and sunglasses, he just stood there, watching.

"I saw him in the Hotel Grande stalking a waiter like a jaguar does his prey," said Philip. "But it was best not to say so in a loud voice, because the slightest thing would offend him, and he then he would pull out his knives. Imagine him on a rickety cot, butt cheeks facing up above a rug rat bent underneath his weight, his hands like pliers on a child's delicate ribs. Crunchy cannibal coitus. Like a scorpion devouring a grasshopper completely, feet, wings, and all. Just picture it."

26

SEX IN THE MARKET

Gabriel Jasón had seen her in the market palpitating the fruit, examining green tomatoes, Canarian chiles, flowers on trays, and stones carved in the form of the Heim classification of *Psylocibe mexicana*—which looked like erect dancing phalluses wearing hats in the shape of foreskins or like defeated penises when they were withered. Gabriel followed her through the passageways and the stalls as she bought San José bread, a kilo of Café Oro, and tortillas tlayudas from the women who made them to order. He observed her from behind as she stared at the clock tower in front of the cathedral of San Juan Evangelista. He sat in front of her in a café while she read a book about film noir. From what he could infer, she liked mystery movies and criminal capers, because she would draw checkmarks next to the movies from the 1940s with red lipstick: *The Maltese Falcon, The Killers, Gilda,* and *The Big Sleep*. Even when she was alone, seemingly bored, he didn't approach her. He was intimidated by her beauty and her distinguished bearing, and he, clumsy, unkempt, and starving, felt unpresentable in comparison. But something about her fascinated him, her brown eyes above all, or maybe it was her indifference, which reminded him of the naked woman lying on the waves in the painting *The Water Nymphs* by Paul Delvaux. Though he also compared her to his *Sleeping Venus.*

"If possible, I would like you to accompany me on a trip. What trip? A trip on *Psylocibe mexicana*," he said to himself in front of the church as a procession came up behind him carrying a crucified Christ wearing a straitjacket, eyes popping out of his skull, arms akimbo. On the way to the altar, a healer asked in a song that there be light in the world.

After midnight, the young *extranjera* left María Sabina's shack after participating in her Thursday velada. Gabriel saw that she was tripping, her eyes dilated after ingesting who knows how many pairs of hallucinogenic male and female mushrooms. She had slipped out of the shack after the candles had been blown out, and the darkness concealed her flight. Hidden in the brushwood, he been crouching outside to spy on the ceremony. Even though she passed right by him, she didn't notice him or the sinister figure of a one-eyed healer who was following her, gesticulating, obviously inebriated. The one-eyed man, it was said, had gone mad because he didn't respect the rule of sexual abstinence that the mushrooms demanded five days before and five days after eating them. The man's nagual was a green iguana that wandered through the trees with a red kerchief around his neck.

Like a lost soul, the young woman descended from Cerro del Fortín, weaving through the brushwood. From his hiding place, Gabriel Jasón watched her blond hair floating against her spine. It wasn't until she turned around in the street that he saw her hair was almost white. She looked like the Bride of Frankenstein resuscitated by a demented doctor to be a spouse for his monster.

Gabriel Jasón was a man lying in wait. He pretended to examine the phases of the moon as he followed his wandering prey. He watched her enter the windowless and doorless bus terminal, where at this hour there was only one passenger bus parked with its lights turned off. He waited for her at the exit when she would pass through a tunnel that smelled of urine and gasoline.

She went into the marketplace and walked through the passageways, between the stalls covered with tarps and newspapers. Perhaps feeling pursued by this stranger, she then tried to head back to María Sabina's shack.

Lost among the market stalls, he watched her draw closer, then move away and walk in circles, like a figure in a dream that goes in and out of their body. And after reciting to her a few García Lorca verses, "Aquella noche corrí / el mejor de los caminos, / montado en potra de nácar / sin bridas y sin estribos . . . ," he proceeded to attack her and strip her clothes off. Jasón threw her over a tiny spice stall, between a crate of green tomatoes and a pipe to which were tied a turkey and a goat waiting to be killed. Using all of his force, he bent her over, and holding her wrists, he penetrated her. All this while trying to pull her hair out of his mouth, to not swallow the cream of her cheeks, and struggling to keep his balance and not fall to the floor, which was covered in trays of flowers and boxes of cilantro. Dominated and enveloped by his hands and thighs, she scratched at him. "You rip me open with your penis, I rip you open with my nails and my teeth," she howled in halting Spanish.

"I am lightning, trapped. You trapped me and enchanted me with your thighs. When I remove myself from you, like lightning I will traverse the world in downpour and gales," he responded, covered in hair and blood.

The breaking dawn roused Gabriel, as the proprietors and vendors began walking down to the market along steep paths and opening the store shutters. These men wore white clothing and hats and were accompanied by women in huipiles embroidered with red birds.

Gabriel gave Ivanna a stalk of gladiola that he'd stolen from a bucket. "To file down the roughness," he said. She stood up and wrapped her head in a red kerchief. They remained frozen, as if bolted to the floor, until they began to hear footsteps around them.

"Tell me your name," he begged.

"Ivanna." She extricated herself from his arms and headed out to the main street.

Gabriel walked toward the hotel seeing nothing besides a pair of brown eyes and a pair of pink nipples on an empty street (even though it was actually packed with of people).

27

BRAIDS SHINING IN THE GLOOM

Howard and Guadalupe passed a decrepit sports field overgrown with thorny weeds and undergrowth. In the central circle was a coffee plant. The line in the middle of the field was made up of rocks; same with the corner kick points. In the goal box, the goalie was a scarecrow. A soccer ball lay deflated to one side, and a player's lone boot, missing its laces, lay far below. The Benito Juárez stadium project had been cast aside by its construction crew. The members of the local tequío, or work commune, had abandoned its construction with the same enthusiasm with which they undertook it. The work, which was to last one full Sunday, had been approved by the local authorities and those who attended the market in the main plaza. They had decreed that the facility would become the home of the local team, Los Tigres Mazatecos.

José Venancio told Howard and Guadalupe that on the day of the job, neighbors from all over the vicinity of Río Tonto had gathered together the most able men to participate in the construction and then baptized the site by beating horns and shells. He said that upon reaching the edge of the town, the men, carrying the building materials on their backs, had broken into a run, yelling and racing to be the first to occupy the site. He said that they all heard in their imaginations the roar of the audience from the stands, cheering on the local *fútbolistas* in the imagined defeat of their rivals on opening day. Such a shame, continued José Venancio, that the installation of the stands was never completed. The bricks collapsed, and in place of imagined fútbolistas running over the grass, you just heard the wind, the wide-mouthed wind coming down from the mountains.

The last the Huautlacos saw of this magnum opus was a job during Holy Week, when the locals were summoned by the municipal president to bring a huge number of large tree trunks to encircle the playing field. The volunteers, in groups of twenty, transported the heavy logs through the streets, balancing them precariously on their shoulders. But then the ropes broke, the trunks plunged down the town's steep staircases, and the great day of the Mazatec Tigers and their fans never came to be.

When Guadalupe and Howard arrived at María Sabina's house, they didn't want to disturb the ceremony that was underway, so they joined in silently. It was Thursday, and the mycologists, the foragers, and the beatniks, a group unto themselves, had all been there for more than two hours. All with the intention of observing the preliminaries of the sacred mushroom rite.

Apolonia translated for her mother: "María Sabina says the altar is like a boat with legs representing the earth, the air, the water, and fire. In a corner of the room is a drum without a bottom and a violin without strings, as the music is resting."

"Where are you from?" Philip asked the priestess of the mushrooms.

"My mother says: 'From the past.' Her ancestors taught her to observe the planet Venus, Citlálpol, 'the great star,' and from the Tonalpohuqui priests, the counters of days, she learned to divide time into threads of fifty-two years, with each thread representing one cycle of forgetting."

Apolonia continued after a pause: "Her ancestors celebrated a holiday in which masked dancers, dressed as animals and plants, danced with live serpents in the dance of the goddess Xochiquétzal, the quetzal flower, celebrating the sexual power of the maiden."

"Those are your origins?"

"My origins aren't specific to me, they are the origins of my town. The Mazatec live in the states of Oaxaca and Puebla. We eat what we grow: maize, beans, squash, sugarcane, coffee, chocolate, and tobacco ... We wear clothes that we weave, skirts and huipiles embroidered with animal and plant motifs."

"Do your people practice *nagualismo?*"*

"We respect the jaguar, the eagle, the serpent, and the crocodile. Some sorcerers believe that they can even become these animals."

"And the healers?"

"They are descendants of the old Tonalpohuqui from Teotitlán del Camino."

"Your braids shine in the twilight."

"We bring out the shine of our hair by rubbing it with the oil of seed of the *pixtle,* or mamey fruit. Our women are famously short, but we live up in the high mountains."

"You never learned to speak Spanish?"

"Not to read or write, but since I was a girl, since I first tried the mushrooms, I've spent my life reading the mysteries of life."

"Your favorite holiday?"

"María Sabina says," intervened Herlinda, "'It's the festival of darkness, celebrated during Holy Week in the church of San Juan Evangelista. Then the women stand in the doorways of their homes frantically beating gourds with little sticks. More and more they beat them, faster and faster, until the people in the church, with all the candles and lights extinguished, begin to stamp and yell so that the bad spirits depart. If you wish,' she says, 'when Easter comes, I'll take you to witness the ceremony.'"

"I don't know if we will still be here," replied Philip.

*In Mesoamerican mythology, a nagual is either a person or shaman who can shift into animal form or an animal guardian spirit. *Nagualismo* is the generalized belief in naguals.

Outside the shack, Gabriel Jasón started to rock out silently.

"Please calm yourself. Your frenzied stomping is disturbing the Principal Beings," the teacher Herlinda came over and said.

"The mayor isn't trustworthy. In Teotitlán del Camino he is the proprietor of a dive bar full of trafficked Tehuana women with a pimp whose nickname is El Popoluca. He gets them drunk on aguardiente and makes them dance naked in the dark for their clients," Miss Pike whispered into Philip's ear when the face of the mayor emerged in the half-light.

"I'd like to see that," said Gabriel Jasón.

28

"SIX WAYS OF LOOKING AT A COLD NIGHT"

"It's raining outside. Inside the walls are wet. The cold air enters through the cracks, under the doors, and penetrates the thin panes of glass that shake at the slightest touch.

"The cold gets through gloves, masks, socks, wool shirts that the guests wear to protect themselves from the weather and to keep themselves warm.

"The night stiffens the sheets, covers, overcoats, the blankets, and the pillows. The rooms have undergone a strange change, as if Dante's Inferno was not a burning hell but a series of frozen circles and the punishment of the damned consisted of icicles torturing a body that is eternally cold.

"It is the time of the frosts, of the cold that burns. It seems like the room has no roof and that a spider with frozen feet is lowering itself out of the darkness of the night onto the faces of the sleeping.

"To go to the bathroom, it is necessary to armor yourself in sweaters and quilts and then to behold your misery with black eyes in the mirror as you clean the frost from your stiffened hair. The body shivers just looking at the blue of the cold out the windows.

"Upon waking in the dark, the eyelids are heavy with dew, the hands frozen stiff by the touch of the harsh air, the walls are rigid. Barbara doesn't dare to stick even one foot out of bed, she doesn't dare to step on tiles so frozen that the cold penetrates socks and shoes. Even the humidity that rises from the ground cuts through them."

On the following day, in a velada, after eating the landslide mushrooms, Philip wrote in his notebook "Six Ways of Looking at a Cold Night." He intended to send the text to Kenneth Rexroth, so he put it into an envelope, scrawled an address on it, searched for a little store where they sold stamps, and then threw the card in the mailbox. He felt weighed down by an indescribable, strange sadness, as much on paper as internally, as if cheer and depression both would just end up in the basket of forgetting.

These were his feelings as he headed to the market with Barbara to meet Howard at doña Anita's food stall. But at the entrance to the market, he ran into María Sabina.

"Last night I saw you in the cold of the night," she said via Apolonia. "You were in my dream. What were you wandering around doing at that time, lost in Cerro del Fortín? Was it really you or someone who looked like you? You had a pale, listless, bored look. *Mhmhmhmh. Tsotsotsotso.*"

"It was me, because I dreamed that I crossed paths with you that night after eating mushrooms in your house during a velada. We could call that surprise meeting an arranged appointment."

"At the same time as you said, I also ran into you on the shore of the Río Santiago. It was at midnight with a sunny moon, cold. The current of the river was fast and strong; its surface undulated like the Mexican flag. You watched the fish jump with frozen eyes. *Tsotsotsotso.*" María Sabina watched him strangely, as if she had not seen him for a long time, despite the fact that he had just visited her recently.

"We had a conversation about the water." María Sabina, speaking all of a sudden in Spanish (in the dream), had said: "Look at the green waves flowing next to the red waves, look at the braids shining in the blue of the cold."

"Notice the darkness of the water, as if it had a soul, as if that soul was liquid and frozen. I don't know how to explain it, but the water that departs and the water that returns was a water that watched sidelong, a water that dreamed, a water that spoke, a water that was mine," said Philip.

"That was what I said about the water you dreamed," said María Sabina and left.

"How many do you want?" asked Barbara upon seeing him approach the table at the market.

"What are you talking about?"

"Grasshopper tacos in sauce. Collected in the cornfields, fried in oil, and served with garlic and salsa with pajarito chiles. They're delicious."

"If you like grasshopper tacos. How gross," Philip muttered when doña Anita put on the table a dish of green-glazed clay filled with the golden insects. Barbara wrapped them in a warm tortilla and began to eat them. Not only did they crunch between her teeth, but they also jumped inside of her mouth.

"How can you eat grasshoppers?" Philip got up from the table and offered his plate to an old, toothless man with incredulous eyes who had been watching him turn down what he considered an exquisite delicacy.

"Does the poet prefer red ants in black mole?" asked doña Anita.

"I would prefer to eat air," he responded.

29

IVANNA'S TRIP

"The desert doesn't just have one voice. It has many voices that the wind carries back and forth. You don't just hear it once; it has several echoes and words. It's a music of sand." Ivanna was seated at a table in the restaurant at the Hotel Grande, telling Gabriel Jasón about how she had arrived at Huautla de Jiménez along with her father, Nicholas Gordon, and her mother, Tatiana, on an expedition they had referred to as "the search for the magic mushroom." Also traveling with them was Roger Hofmann, the eminent chemist from the laboratories of Sandoz in Basel, Switzerland, who had worked on the formula for psilocybin, and a photographer, Richard Stevenson.

"Tell me all the details," said the Chilean, who, always eager for new experiences or at least to hear about the adventures of others, was watching her like he might eat her words with his eyes.

"We crossed the mountains in central northern Oaxaca then, because the mushrooms appear at the beginning and the end of the rainy season. I had just turned sixteen years old, and it was my first trip outside of school. In Tehuacán, the city of water, I saw a head thrown in the dust, the face split in two, and I carried it from bus to bus like a talisman. My father told me to throw it away, as I would definitely find a more interesting toy at one of the stone altars erected in the peaks of Cerro Rabón by the ancient Mazatec, where the Principal Beings lived."

"How did you make the trip?"

"We crossed the mountain range in a second-class bus, a rundown vehicle that took us to abandoned terminals in the middle of parched fields. Traveling with Mazatec passengers weighted down with sacks, turkeys, and goats on dirt roads, we finally found refuge with Julia Martínez, an innkeeper who was as fat as the fat cacique from Cempoala.* A while later, we arrived at dawn in a town perched on the outskirts of the mountain range. We were all starving, broken, and in need of a bath. We were in Huautla, where Herlinda Martínez Cid, the teacher in the town, greeted us from the doorway of her house."

"Could you make out Cerro Rabón?"

"The outline of Cerro Rabón was visible from a distance, because it's two thousand feet above sea level. Seeing it cheered us up. My father said that the Mazatec called it that because its tail was cut by a lightning bolt. They think it is a sacred mountain because the spirits of the hills and the waters and Father Sun, Father Thunder, and Mother Moon all live in its caves."

"It's a zone of eroding earth, branching cliffs, and wind canyons where unrealized dreams live."

"I remember that when we passed a gorge frequented by bandits, the mule driver Óscar Wilde Gómez (whose father chose his name from a magazine) pointed out four corpses hanging in the trees, then placed his hand on his gun and told us that the bandits would wait to attack until after the party was worn out by the climb." Ivanna sat thinking while the waiter brought over some beers. "When we crossed the Río Tonto, we saw an Indian man leading down a pack of mules carrying coffee sacks. The funny thing was that La Muerte was driving the mule driver with her sharp lashes just as he was driving the mules.

*A reference to Xicomecoatl, the cacique, or ruler, of Cempoala and one of the first Indigenous allies of Hernan Cortés, according to Bernal Díaz del Castillo.

It rained dust in those bald hills, and there wasn't even one tree to rest the eyes on, only rocky ground, rough scenery, only people with blurred features. The shacks were enveloped in mist. At the threshold of a rural store, the locals lined up dressed in white clothing, hand-woven shirts, woven palm hats, and tire-soled huaraches waiting for their daily wages."

"And what of the landscape?"

"I came to appreciate the richness of the mountain biology, from its blue peaks rising more than twenty-five hundred meters above sea level to the ceiba, the mother tree that has its roots in the underworld, its trunk on the surface, and its foliage in heaven. I was tricked by the entrance to the town of the mushrooms. The first thing you see on the path is a street that leads down one hill and is set into another. One pass between the hills leads to another, leads to another, leads to others, which lead to others, until we reached sugarcane fields, orchards of orange trees, and coffee plantations, all with adobe walls behind them, and behind those, the abyss," continued Ivanna. "At the recommendation of Óscar Wilde, we stayed in the house of the teacher Herlinda, friend of the missionary Pike, the only foreigner who spoke Mazatec and who offered to translate the songs of María Sabina into English. Although she didn't believe in the mushrooms."

"How did it happen with María Sabina?"

"One night the shaman celebrated the rite of the Teonanácatl for us," said Dr. Roger Hofmann, who had appeared in the restaurant with her father.

"What is the *Psilocybe mexicana*?" asked Jasón. "Isn't the mushroom the Mazatec call the Little Angel just an organism lacking in chlorophyll and tissue that looks like dark worms and grows in the cornfields or dances on the edge of the arroyos?"

Dr. Hoffman answered, "I've seen the *Psilocybe caerulescens* in the husks of sugarcane. You can be sure that the eyes of the mushrooms are blind, but we know that they see. They don't have feet or wings, but they make anyone who ingests them fly. Those that grow at the edge of the land are the flesh of the earth. María Sabina has said that before there was sugarcane here, the landslides could be found in deforested areas."

"What is a mushroom? It's freedom imprisoned. The shocks this organism contains belie its rebellious character." Hofmann picked one up between his fingers and began to shred it.

"The landslide mushroom is like a wild horse when a novice rider tries to mount it," explained Gordon.

"Their form speaks," exclaimed Tatiana. "Phallic, furred, sensual, with or without caps, what beauties."

"What plants know, what plants hear, what plants dream is an enigma worthy of Zeno," interjected Hofmann. "I would like to see a sunflower's dance in my mind."

"Do you remember the numinous? The perception of God in daily life?" asked Gordon. "According to Rudolf Otto, the mode for expressing the numinous is the terrible, the miraculous, what is not understood and what is understood, the darkness and the void."

"Whosoever does not discover the numinous in the mushroom will gain nothing from the sound, song, and word. No ceremony reveals *the living voice of the sacred* as inherently as the hallucinogenic mushroom's nature."

"Beatniks heading straight for us," said Tatiana. "Don't wave at them. It will give them a reason to come over to the table."

"It's Philip and Barbara."

"I don't care." Hofmann turned to face the window.

"José Venancia told me that in the middle of the night he heard the steps of María Sabina descending Cerro del Fortín on the street to the market," continued Gordon without paying attention to those present. "The sound of her bird feet stepping over the wooden logs."

"I told you, because in the voice of her steps you can discover the presence of the dead who refuse to leave," said Hofmann.

"Quiet, the Holy Children I've eaten are sleeping in my stomach." Tatiana offered Philip and Barbara a seat and a drink of aguardiente.

30

THE EXPERIENCE OF WATER

In the hour between two lights, María Sabina was seated on a stone in the brushwood, her head just visible above the thicket. Her braids hung down, woven with ribbons, and she was smoking a cigar. Not far from her an old horse was eating corn kernels scattered in the grass. Behind her the image of a Mazatec calendar with three concentric circles was carved on a rock. The circles were pierced by three hundred small lines, representing the days. According to archaeologists, the ancients had built a temple in this place dedicated to the cult of the dog god, "the nagual Xolotl, the name of the god of fire." The dog god had broken the straps binding him, thanks to a priest who had not respected the rule of sexual abstinence, and had transformed into hundreds of wild dogs who then overran the markets, the streets, and the towns in search of food.

A little later María Sabina spied a man without eyes in a green cap and tattered clothes crossing a hanging bridge. The man, with his arms open wide, looked like a parrot about to break into flight, though he was probably just trying to balance himself as he teetered across the Río Tonto.

Later still, María Sabina's eyes passed over the meeting point between the Río Amapa and Río Tonto, where she spied a couple of foreigners (Philip and Barbara) in the shadow of Father Sol and Father Trueno's residence. According to tradition, there was an enchanted lake at the summit of Cerro Rabón, where whales, sea turtles, and monsters with golden eyes had been seen, as well as a gourd of seven colors, and inside of that was where the rainbow was created by the four directional winds. It was believed that one could hear the booming of thunder that proceeded the earthquakes there a few times a day. The noise came from a place in the east where an ancient one sat on top of the sea and whose enormous breasts fed the cornfields. The noise happened when she nursed them, which then made the leaves whisper. This ancient one, given the name of Shumajé, or "Great Thunder," began to wane during the ninth month and continued growing smaller and smaller. If one sowed in that time, the cornfields would not flourish.

Standing on the blue-green hill, the two beatniks seemed not only insubstantial, but transparent. Before slipping into a cave there, Philip felt the gaze of María Sabina on his back and turned in the direction of where she was. A yellow dog appeared at his side, so skinny it looked like a drawing of Xolotl, the dog god.

When Philip and Barbara arrived at the velada around eleven that night, they found the mother and daughter seated in the kitchen. María Sabina kept her eyes closed but moved her lips as if she was speaking to herself or as if she was in conversation with creatures invisible to the naked eye.

"Will you stay for the velada?" asked Apolonia, lighting the candles and hanging images of the Virgin Mary over the altar on the table.

"Gift yourself a vision." Tatiana passed in front of them with a basket of landslide mushrooms. "I am tempted, but I have a fear of the unknown."

"It's not the same, the blind eye of the water and the eye of water that watches us when we drink," said María Sabina. "When one consumes the God Meat, the Holy Children travel from one vision to another, from one tongue to another, from one mystery to another."

"María Sabina says," said Miss Herlinda, the teacher, "'Look at the water boiling on the stove, dissolving into bubbles. Up from the depths of its combustion, from the depths of itself, it speaks, look. Say what you will, your vision burns.'"

"Listen to the river of the mind that flows iridescent and filled with light, because as Cayetano García says, an eye of water is not the same as the water's eye," Roger Hofmann interjected from out of the darkness. "Its waves become pupils that watch you discreetly, intensely. When its bubbles become eyes, they reflect not just a time that has passed but also a time you can glimpse through the water."

"María Sabina says," said Miss Herlinda, the teacher, "'Looking at water refreshes my eyes; its liquid hands wash my face; its transparency trickles down my cheeks, enters my mouth, scrutinizes my innards, mixes with my thoughts, flows a current of images through my self.'"

"At any moment the eye of the water returns to the blind river that glides within the river of time. One thing is sure, my eyes see the world more clearly than before," added Roger. "I see the visible bubbles of water in front of my eyes, and lodging myself in them, I feel like I will never go back to seeing them as empty sockets."

"I see the eyelids of the water opening, the water opening its eyes." Gordon tried not to spray the others with words enveloped in spit. The sound of his voice was rasping, as if his larynx was irritated. "I see the colorless water, the odorless water, the intangible water, the fugitive water."

"María Sabina says," said the teacher Herlinda, "'The mystery of the water has been revealed. The water lives, the water senses, the water sees.'"

From the shadows María Sabina sung:

I am the woman light
I am the woman who births light
I am the woman moon
I am woman water
Santo, santo, santo

31

GERHART IN THE CANTINA

Some drunks seated against the white wall in the cantina watched through the window as outside the inebriated German clawed at stones and pulled up the grass.

Two Mazatec youths grabbed him to bring him home; he had become belligerent and because of that had been taken outside. As they wrestled him out, Gerhart Münch admired the cheekbones of his captors, which made them look like they had no eyes. But this vision was just part of his delirium. Until the owner of the cantina had ordered his comrades in inebriation, who had shared many bottles of mezcal and aguardiente with him, to throw him out in the street and shut the door behind him, Gerhart had thought them handsome.

A taxi driver parked to the side of the bus terminal and in front of the bar watched the young men carrying the musician in their arms. He was so inebriated that he played "Musical Moments" by Schubert in the air. He attempted to free himself from his captors and run. But he wasn't just drunk on alcohol, he was also drunk on melancholy and frustration. Daily, with a Teutonic punctuality, he self-destructed. "I humiliate and I destroy myself," he said, parodying Walt Whitman.

"Hello," he greeted Philip and Barbara with his marked German accent. "I invite you to invite me for a drink."

It was the magic hour in Huautla: the sky was resplendent. In the local store, lit up with the economic glow of forty-watt light bulbs, Vera made her purchases for the weekend: two hundred grams of coffee, a bottle of aguardiente, a fourth of a kilo of Oaxacan cheese, a package of María biscuits, four candles to light the kitchen, a headless chicken, and, for Gerhart's hangover, a bottle of Sal de Uvas Picot—a laxative, aperitif, antacid, digestive, and diuretic, according to the advertisement. And as a gift from the Bubblemaid, a Mexican moon-faced pixie used to market the product, the storekeeper handed her a musical compilation, *Cancionero Picot 1956*.

Vera bought all of this on credit at La Gallega grocery store while outside Gerhart staggered under the sun, his trembling hands scratching at the air. With his one eye, he watched who entered and who left and, above all, whether they carried something he could drink. By his anxious face one could see he was equally capable of drinking a flask of perfume, a bottle of tequila, or a liter of turpentine.

"Hello," he greeted Philip and Barbara. "What brings you to these lands of God?"

"We're just out strolling."

"I'm drunk."

"We see."

"I pawned the piano."

"We're sorry."

"I owed money to the bartender."

"How much?"

"A hundred meters of hope and five hundred moons of beans."

"How long did you owe him for?"

"Since we arrived in Huatla I haven't paid my debts for cups, bottles, flasks, nips."

Vera clarified: "Exhibiting his Germanic discipline, Gerhart toasts a tribute to Bacchus every day with aguardiente, mezcal, tequila, beer. At five in the afternoon, the mountains waver in front of his one eye, and the twilight sways through the hills. In such moments of total inebriation, his body collapses among the weeds and loose rocks, and the whole world makes him stumble. That taxi driver parks near the bar and, like an asshole, refuses to drive us because he's afraid my husband will urinate on the seat or, worse, that he won't pay when he's dropped off."

"That's why my dear Vera has no alternative but to carry me and bear my thirst for self-destruction. She is so afraid that if she lets me go, I'll run to a bar and order tequila, perfume, even turpentine to drink, so she sinks her claws into my ribs and she holds my wrists with more strength than a Viking in heat. At home, our drunk friend throws himself pitilessly on the Agua de Colonia and the perfume atomizers, but he finds out in desperation that I'd already drunk them all yesterday."

"Good luck with that." Philip and Barbara bid them farewell.

"Good afternoon, lady and sir. Do you perhaps remember me? According to a rigorous hierarchy, I am the third assistant of the teacher Herlinda Martínez Cid. I want to advise you—for no extra charge, let's be clear about that—on your purchases of local arts and crafts. I would love to take you to the market where the special of the day today is a stone mushroom in the shape of a phallus." When the two had entered the hotel, they had run into Rosalindo Flores in the lobby. She had been waiting with a magazine in hand, and upon seeing them enter, she sprang up out of her seat to greet them.

32

THE BEATNIKS GATHER

When the sun went down, Philip and Barbara arrived at the bar on the plaza.

"Our own Gato Rojo," he said.

"Our own dirty table." Barbara gestured at the table with glasses of beer and cups of mezcal containing dried worms.

"I would like you to meet the parishioners who never take their eyes off the gringos, especially you with your tight pants and low-cut top."

"What can I serve you? Aguardiente or mezcal?" A skinny, flat-chested waitress without hips or ass approached the table.

"The house aguardiente."

"Every time I bring you a round of drinks, you'll need to pay. Not because I don't trust you—it's the owner's orders," said the waitress.

"We'd like the same," ordered Guadalupe, who had just arrived that moment along with Howard, Gabriel Jasón, and Ivanna.

"There is another area for women to sit."

"We'll stay here. We're a couple."

The waitress left, scandalized.

"Beatific vacations, that's what I call my stay in Huautla," said Guadalupe. "During the mornings I take classes in Mazatec with Miss Pike, and in the afternoons I come drink mezcal in the cantina holding Howard's hand, just like a Huichol on peyote barreling down Cerro del Fortín, not stopping until he reaches the very edge of his self."

"Just like *Wanderer Above the Sea of Fog* by Caspar David Friedrich, I am intoxicated by the panorama," Howard confided.

"We've been undone by the storm that lashes the mountains, more so by the nostalgia it inspires within us," said Philip.

"We must create our lives, not just graze on the days. We should discover the woman, not just make her fat." Gabriel looked at Ivanna. "When I was a boy, mouth open, I wanted to eat the whole breast, ha ha. But now the mediocre, the sterilized, who waste their days in factories and offices, want to use a schedule to murder my limitless desire and my fierce joy."

"The day I met María Sabina, even as the darkness came and covered me from head to toe, I understood death. But she didn't feel it, just heard the *tap tap* of shadows," said Ivanna.

"But, ha ha, tell me, my friends, who are those sons of bitches watching us from the other table? Definitely police. Ha ha."

"Guadalupe drives me crazy with her smooth crotch, her parted lower lip. I love to lie on her womb and doze off while gazing at her slumped moons."

"Howard likes to read Chinese poetry intermittently while also watching the shadow of my nakedness projected on the wall by a red lampshade," Guadalupe admitted.

"I possess no objects or mementos. My treasures are all alive and kicking in front of my eyes," said Gabriel Jasón.

"At midnight I love her sex cocktails, her kisses that taste like tequila and inspire violence and lust beyond all reason," Howard exclaimed.

"Man, you can't deny that you suffer from sexual hallucinations and that she has an irresistible sex appeal and all the rest."

"OK. Who put on this jazz station playing Charlie Parker?" asked Barbara.

"I did," said Philip.

"Careful, those three sitting at the table next to us are watching us and listening. They must be federal agents—they haven't taken their eyes or their attention off us for a second," Gabriel warned.

"Which ones?" asked Ivanna, turning to look at some local drunks sitting in the corner.

"No, not those ones. The ones maintaining some sort of austere silence, like they're at a Mass."

"Excuse me, my name is the spirit of the oldest balladeer," Philip had begun to write, his face toward the window.

"What will you title your poem?" asked Gabriel Jasón after a bit.

"Ballad of the Muses and the Furies."

Tell me, you vagabonds,
In what country, cemetery, or crematory
Does Lucille rest, the tailor of the black dress,
Of El Palacio de las Malas Artes,
In what dump is Barbara lost,
The Sanfranciscan of arms
Who has to walk 'til dawn
The street of San Juan de Letrán,
Her leonine hair, breasts loose
Under her grimy white blouse,
Where she meets the gay pair, Allen and Lucien,
Dressed as women, drinking the words
Of Buddha and Rimbaud.
Where have the muses and the furies gone,
Who, walking under the serpent sun
With their weed in a bag, books in a backpack,
Boy Scout knife in hand,
Lose themselves in a labyrinth of words,
Searching for bliss.

"What's up, muchachos?" All of a sudden, a policeman was standing at their table, blue shirt unbuttoned and a cigarette in his hand, dropping ash.

"We're gathering," Gabriel Jasón explained.

"Gathering, huh. Passing the weed from mouth to mouth, huh?" The federal agents also walked over to join the group.

"This is a place for men. Women drink in the annex," said one of them.

"The owner doesn't care," the waitress chimed in.

"Well, we do. It's the rules. Understand?" said another.

"Rules matter to me," responded Gabriel Jasón. "Since I was thirteen years old, I declared myself an independent country free of priests, rabbis, imams, and pastors."

"How macho. Do us a favor and clear out of here, huh? If you don't follow the law, you'll end up spending the night behind bars. Best pay and be off."

33

THE CAVE

The river flowed along the sides of the mountains to wash the feet of the Lord of the Hills. When the countryfolk standing at its edge were asked the name of this river, they responded, "River." When he heard this answer, Philip said to himself that the pre-Hispanic artists tracing the flow of the waters over the cave walls were trying to freeze not only time but also the instant of its flight.

Early in the morning, with bags of food and water, straw hats to keep off the sun, and battery-operated lanterns, he and Barbara rented a taxi outside the market and directed its driver toward the town of San Agustín. They arrived a half an hour later, the taxi's headlights dark, as the car's fuse box was defective and kept flickering on and off.

A doctor, Nancy Edam, and a speleologist, John Powell, were waiting there, ready for the excursion. Originally from Minnesota, they'd been studying the Huautla cave system for years, a complex cavern that was the largest in the Americas and that consisted of a web of vaults and stone rooms, a number of underground bodies of water, pools, waterfalls, and sacred hills and mountains. Howard and Guadalupe came pedaling along the path on bicycles. Ivanna and Gabriel arrived with a bag of turkey tacos, black mole, and soft drinks.

"I can't wait to enter into the subterranean world. I want to touch the invisible water and discover the compressed light in the ancient darkness," said Gabriel.

"What are you doing here?" asked Powell.

"We're searching for bliss," said Howard. "Our eyes are hungrier than our stomachs," he added.

"I thought . . . ," Guadalupe started to say.

"In the cave one shouldn't think, one should pay attention to where they are stepping," interjected Dr. Edam.

"Ever since I learned of the Huautla cave system, I wanted to subsume my whole self in the virgin material of the cave. I am in agony over the possibility of disappearing from my companion's eyes without being invisible, to wrap my three-dimensional body in the blackness," Gabriel explained.

"And you, what's your reasoning?" Powell asked Philip and Barbara.

"The hope of illuminating ourselves within the darkness of the cave," Philip responded.

"At fifteen hundred meters below the surface?"

"And more."

"The people of this place find this type of study not only sacrilegious but also terrifying. They believe that there is a point in the complex where the Lord of the Caves will seal off the intruder's passage so they not only can become lost but might even be killed."

"That's the point to which we want to go."

"Are you sure? You can die in the trying; we will not be responsible for your safety."

"We assume all the risk."

"I am Tobías Rocha. I hope that you will all be comfortable in the cave." From one of the numberless entrances to the cave, a scrawny man with small, sharp eyes emerged. "Don't worry, I am the guide recommended by Miss Pike."

"The señora María Sabina says that if there was a nuclear war, we could save ourselves from the nuclear fallout caused by the rain of bombs by hiding in this cave. It provides the perfect conditions for surviving a third world war," said Dr. Edam.

"María Sabina knows the cave as well as her own hand. She believes that we could spend one hundred years hidden inside it. And that in this inverted Babel that could accommodate millions of people, we would survive until global radiation passed," added Powell.

"The healers of Huautla recommend that visitors abstain from sexual relations five days before and seven days after penetrating the seven layers of the interior world," said Tobías.

"The first level is the level of the lunar rain, the second is the belt of star eyes belonging to the goddess Citlalicue, she of the skirt of stars, also known as the Milky Way. The third level belongs to Tonatiuh, god of the sun. The fourth is the territory of the deity of salt water. The fifth, that of the star arrows, or the place of the meteorites," explained Powell.

"In the sixth the god of death reigns. The supreme level. Omeyocan. It is the place of duality or of the god of two," Dr. Edam concluded.

"There are caves so gloomy that even when bathed in sunlight they seem shut off and dark. Not only are their interiors impenetrable, but in their surrounding areas, the locals treat visitors with outright hostility," Powell informed them.

"I who arrived at adulthood as an exhibitionist, in this darkness, cannot see myself," said Jasón.

"Guadalupe doesn't feel her body, she took opium," Howard revealed.

"Good for her," joked Powell.

"To think that when stepping out of the bus, the second I arrived in Huautla I delighted in the nakedness of the grass, and now I follow a strange material of smeared green on my shoes like I have stepped on lizards." Jasón led the way.

"How long have you known each other?" Dr. Edam asked Barbara.

"Good question."

"Why?"

"Philip and I met in El Gato Rojo, but I don't think it was the first time we'd seen each other. I myself don't even know how long I've been inside myself."

"What does that mean?"

"Sometimes the last meeting happened in another life, or the first, you never know."

"Do you remember something particular?"

"Only that a long time ago I touched his fading hand on a bed."

"And?"

"Now I return to embrace it. Even though his body has another skin color, his face is different, his way of looking is the same."

"When were you born?"

"I know the actual date of my birth, but not the dates of my previous births. The memories assault me; my ancient memory attacks me constantly. And for that reason, I doubt my present. I am older than I look; my life can't be measured in years but in ages. In my fantasies I feel like a centenarian, millionarian, immensely old. The dream of life is kept in an empty box."

"How tedious."

"Why?"

"Like in *Dracula,* how tedious to drink from a new neck every night and every morning be thirsty again."

"Am I interrupting?" interrupted Tobías. "In this place it is believed that at this particular time of year, you can hear from another part of the cave a boom of thunder like that which proceeds an earthquake, and that the sound comes from a place where an ancient woman sits on the sea. There is a book that says this ancient one has huge breasts that she uses to feed the cornfields, and when she is giving them milk, the leaves of the corn echo. This ancient one is called Shumajé, which means "Great Thunder." But during the ninth month the woman starts to grow smaller. If one sows in this time, the fields don't grow, because she continues to wane. It's the same with us: as soon as we reach the largest cave, we will also begin to grow smaller and smaller."

"I ask for silence; we don't want to anger the ancient one of the cave with such ruckus." Ivanna turned to Guadalupe, who was shaking with a nervous euphoria.

"We proceed into the first cave. Careful of the illusions of the gods in the Wet Mirror and of interior vertigo." Tobías Rocha crossed over the threshold of the fifteenth entrance.

"What are those things?" Howard stepped on some broken beer bottles and boxes of candles.

"You are walking over the tracks of a mining train that is no longer used. Try not to trip or hit your head. Now we are moving into a room with a vault that has a height of fifty meters."

One after the other the cataphiles followed the subterranean web until they began to lose all sensation of time and place and abandoned themselves to the wisdom of Tobías and the cave. The entrances and exits to this vertical and horizontal labyrinth disconcerted and terrified them, because in the darkness the visitor was equally likely to encounter a slab as an abyss, a crevasse as a black river.

Barbara couldn't see her hands or her feet. She almost ran into a pair of gold discs and didn't know whether they belonged to an animal or a skull on an altar.

"It's an *ocelotl*," said the guide, grabbing her arm and pushing her to keep moving. "By the black spots on its hide, we know it's a spotted jaguar. If it was a *melánico* jaguar, like a panther, it would have been invisible in the dark."

"Did you notice that?" asked Barbara with a shaking voice. "A strong vibration shook my body, and I felt pulled by that animal across space at a great speed. Then I returned to myself without having moved an inch."

"Come here." Guadalupe, with a lantern in hand, illuminated the way.

"Careful, the mate of the feline could be nearby and might attack us," said the guide, pulling them forward.

"What is a *Panthera onca* doing in this place?" asked Powell.

"Fishing for clouds in the sky of the abyss," answered Jasón.

"Where did it come from?"

"Possibly from Tanivet on the way to Mitla. Or from the underworld," Tobías muttered.

"How could it have arrived here?"

"By swimming."

"Is it gone?"

"It's camouflaged against a rock."

"It could be from Monte Albán, whose name in Zapotec means 'Jaguar Hill,' and in Mixtec, 'Hill of the Twenty Jaguars,'" they heard Dr. Edam say from behind.

"I don't know where it came from, but it might be the Lord 12 Jaguar of Mixtec mythology, also known as the Jaguar of the Songs and Coyote of the Knives."

"And the Lord 12 Vulture, the jaguar who assumes the name of Eagle of the Night," Powell chimed in.

"I've seen jaguars in artifacts of stone, clay, in codices and in jade, even in representations of *teyolloquani,* the devourer of human hearts, but I've never been so close to one," mused Dr. Edam.

"I saw a jaguar with four bodies and eight eyes like in the Mural of the Four Eras,"* lied Jasón.

"I didn't know that you knew about cats." Ivanna laughed.

"The jaguar is my nagual."

"Bird Jaguar it was called by the Mayans. Its presence was found in gods, spirits, divine rulers, and ordinary men who attributed their strength to its claws. It is said that every man carries within himself a jaguar and the jaguar is an animal disguised as man," explained Dr. Edam.

"The animal has left, dragging itself away through the water, leaving behind just the sound of its purring," noted Guadalupe.

"Or it became a nagual." Philip looked at Jasón.

*Mural de las Cuatro Eras in Toniná, Chiapas.

34

THE TEMPLE OF IMAGES

When the jaguar disappeared, the party followed its path, leaving behind them a series of tiered passageways and a crevasse filled with water that Tobías had sunk in up to his torso before everyone rushed to help him. Jasón grabbed his hand to pull him to the surface. Two peaks rose out the depths of the aquatic abyss that he had been on the point of falling into. The group continued on until they arrived at a cliff. There, Powell and Edam spread out their instruments in order to measure the tremors in the ground. When they felt tremors, Tobías and the rest laid out on their stomachs to peer below into the bottomless blackness.

"How far is the bottom?" Philip asked Tobías.

"As far as your eyes can imagine it."

Groping through a cavern filled with burials, they came upon a skull decorated with turquoise, covered in the blue-green mineral. Its teeth were rotted away, and it had sunken obsidian eyes.

"This vessel of jade represents a Principal Being, which in turn symbolizes the vital liquids, like those that María Sabina describes in her visions," said Powell.

"No, it isn't." Dr. Edam contradicted him. "It's the image of a priest from another age, a corpse, that appears dead but is outfitted with live currents. We could understand its message if we could capture existential codes from other dimensions. The body that we have in front of us is an open tomb conceived to be visited by us centuries after it was placed here. The Temple of Images has existed for centuries."

"Follow me. I'll take you to a very special place." Tobías Rocha led them toward a stepped alleyway that took them to a pool of water. There they saw a skeleton decorated with turquoise. "This skeleton is a goddess."

"From up close we can see in it its form of a thallophytic plant, lacking chlorophyll, parasitic, moving its body from side to side to stay upright on the ground. Sometimes it represents the *Psilocybe mexicana* that was used during the late preclassical period. In one scene from the bonensis we see the Lord 7 Flower eating hallucinogenic mushrooms while listening to music played by the Lord 9 Wind, in the form of the Mixtec Quetzalcóatl, the divine whirlwind, the Lord with Earflaps in the Form of Snails, or the Lord in Whose Breast Songs Bloom,"* lectured Dr. Edam.

"The huipil with unraveling flowers and birds that falls in rags from the fleshless body belies centuries of use. The wig is a ritual crown; the colorless ribbons surely represent a bond of many years," explained Powell. "From the crown, the hair slips down the spine with its tips pointing downward like the trickles of water off of a stalactite, a signal that it was connected to the Lord of the Caves. We should note also that clinging to the waist is what was once a belt made of pieces of jade, and there was a turquoise mask covering its skull, now covered by petrified mud."

"These five sculptures around the goddess could represent the Principal Beings or the First Beings, the Lords of Black Stone and Colored Stone; the tree lords, the Black Tree Lord and the Green Tree Lord;

*The Codex Vindobonensis Mexicanus I is a screen-fold manuscript from southern Mexico that depicts the deeds of deities and mythological beings. It is one of only a few pictorial documents that survived the preconquest period. The names here are direct translations from the codex text.

the volcano spirits, Ñuhu Earthquake and Ñuhu Burning Stone. As the Codex Vindobonensis says, 'There are beings of great perception, who look forward and look backward, who know the past and the future, who protect and guard. These mysterious beings are the origin of many things.'" Dr. Edam then examined the decorated skulls.

"These skulls could also represent the four cardinal directions and the center, and the sculpture behind her in the form of a mushroom could be her nagual. Or the image of an unknown god," ventured Powell.

"The stone perspires and breathes," commented Philip.

"The detached eyes of the mask turned toward the ground make me uncomfortable. It seems like the empty hollows are watching us," said Barbara, suddenly startled.

"Her open hands seem on the verge of clapping like she was an ancient singer, a primitive priestess of the sacred mushrooms. Or maybe an ancestor of María Sabina. Apart from the epoch in which she lived, it's astonishing how similar she is to her: size, age, appearance," Powell observed.

"This skeleton belongs to a woman of about fifty years of age. The mouth reveals dental inlays now rotted away. On her bones are scratches from the use of bracelets," Dr. Edam continued. "She didn't die in childbirth, she died in a trance. We'll never know what she saw, but by her expression, it was something terrifying."

"At the back of the room, in the dark, you find more Principal Beings. Strange, because it is difficult to find them because of looters. The one behind, with a jadeite body and obsidian eyes, represents the god of young corn, and the one in front, with clear Olmec brushstrokes, an androgynous male similar to the monster Tlaltecuhtli, the earth lord. This masculine/feminine figure might be a god," Powell surmised. "I don't know if you noticed, but at the entrance to the temple are animal remains. I noted a wolf skeleton; it looks like a canine rug spread out over a ritual space for the Principal Beings."

"Let's keep exploring. It will be night soon and we could get lost . . . or run into jaguars and vipers . . . or fall off a cliff. Or scare ourselves with our own shadows." Tobías began walking away.

"In this labyrinth the best plan of action is not to become separated," Dr. Edam recommended.

"We'll come back another day," Powell assured them. "If we keep following the volcano spirits, we will arrive at the jaws of the earth from which human beings emerged."

"What are those creatures?" Myriad eyes gazed at Philip.

"Wolf spiders," shrieked Dr. Edam.

"And the ones that carpet the walls like stars?" asked Barbara.

"Fireflies, Goddess 4 Dog."*

"Look up at the light entering there through a hole." Tobías Rocha pointed at an opening in the dome.

"What's this?" Gabriel shook a cord, which caused hundreds of black bodies clinging to it to fly off.

"Bats!" yelled Powell, the speleologist, and Dr. Edam in unison.

"There goes their god." Gabriel's lantern illuminated an almost phantasmagoric shadow that skimmed along the floor of the cave. "It looks like the finger of death with wings. An evil face, miserable eyes, sharp teeth, furry ears, wrinkled nasal fold, and a membrane of wings like a moving shield. There they go shrieking through the tunnels in search of an exit."

Thousands of bats flew out the entrance to the cave, while inside thousands, maybe millions, more continued to churn. Flurries of them crossed the darkness in whirlwinds of screeching and flapping wings. They crashed into one another, walked and clambered over the clothes and hair of the visitors, and flew flapping overhead. Some even stood on their noses so as look at them face-to-face. Their numbers didn't decrease; even when thousands split off, thousands more watched from the dark with brilliant eyes. One in particular frightened them all as it moved quickly over the black floor like a wingless shadow and then returned to flight, swooping toward the walls while emitting sonic cries. As soon as Tobías yelled, they answered with a deafening sound,

---

*Another reference to an image in the Codex Vindobonensis Mexicanus I.

detaching themselves in bunches, like grapes hanging from the ceiling, walls, and crevices, and raising eddies of dust with their flights.

"Don't antagonize them, they could be hematophagous. Protect your face, arms, and neck," he advised.

"Stay still, don't provoke them. They could attack," Philip counseled Barbara.

"I just want to get out of here," she shrieked.

"Now!" yelled Tobías and the beatniks and the scientists threw themselves toward the exit, stumbling, falling, chased by the cloud of bats, which once outside of the cave dispersed into the brushwood and wetlands, to dizzily hunt insects under the murky sky and disappear into the heart of the night.

35

THE BEATNIKS AND MARÍA SABINA

When the beatniks arrived at María Sabina's house, the mycologists were already there. Apolonia met them at the door.

"Last night my mother saw you enter the Temple of Images in a dream. What were you doing wandering around there? You stood in front of an altar with a human figure seen in its future state. Why would you do that?"

"We went to the cave of Cerro Rabón and came across that altar by accident," Philip explained.

"My mother came upon you by surprise, hiding in the cave, being chased by thousands of bats. What did you do?"

"Nothing. We saw some wolf spiders and fireflies when all of a sudden they rose up like tornadoes from out of their own shit."

"'How strange,' my mother said upon waking last night, 'I dreamed that someone saw me in a dark, frozen place. That they saw me as a shadow of myself, and that it was me and not me at the same time. The voices spoke about me, and when they left, I remained behind in that dark place. How strange that they dreamed me there,'" said Apolonia in the words of her mother.

"How strange," murmured Philip.

"When my mother awoke, she gave thanks to the Principal Beings for the vision, and she went back to sleep. Did anyone take photographs?"

"I took one," Howard revealed.

"You'll have to give us the roll."

"I have it in the hotel."

"We'd like to visit the cave with María Sabina before we go back to New York."

"My mother doesn't like to see herself in the cave, much less in her future form. What else did you see?"

"We saw an ancient woman. Maybe it was her or her ancestor, we don't know," said Philip.

"You shouldn't have seen her."

"It wasn't intentional."

"Apolonia, bring me the mushrooms," María Sabina called to her daughter from the kitchen.

"Is that all you saw?" Gordon interrogated them, bothered. "For that alone you should leave."

"Why?"

"Your discovery bothered the señora. Her presence in the cave is a mystery guarded for over a hundred years . . . or a thousand dreams. Perhaps she lived under a sun that predates ours, the Fourth Sun."

"Gordon's started to hallucinate," Valentina interrupted. "From that thread follows the whole yarn; he'll end up talking about the purple hair of Hades in the Homeric hymn to Demeter."

"Don't tell anyone in town what you saw. Some sorcerer could kill you," ordered Roger.

"Was she the woman at the altar in the cave?" asked Philip.

"Maybe she was the Priestess of the Last Day."

"Generations of tricksters and bohemians, mystics and pessimists, seers and prophets of disaster have passed in front of her, and now it's the turn of the Beats," said Gordon.

"We could explain to the señora what we saw," offered Guadalupe.

"Better to leave it alone. María Sabina is very disturbed. Before that occurred, there was silence."

"Would you like *café de olla?* A drink of aguardiente?" Apolonia emerged from the kitchen holding a clay vessel.

"We're waiting to eat the Little Angels," declared Barbara.

"She is going to begin the ceremony," said Ivanna.

In the room, under the effect of the Holy Children, María Sabina began to dance, clap, and sing.

I am the woman of the cave
I am the body that implodes
I am the woman who sees herself in her future state
And the Codex Vindobonensis, or am I the woman who will be there
Santo, santo, santo

36

THE WEDDING

The sun came out over the Cerro de la Adoración, and the newlyweds, Philip and Barbara, emerged from the white church. Above the pyramidal mountain, the radiant eye illuminated the shadowed town. Richard Stevenson was on the main street when he saw them standing in the doorway of the church of San Juan Evangelista. The two Beats had just gotten married. Barbara wore a huipil embroidered with birds, a yellow clasp in her hair, silver earrings, lips painted with red lipstick, and a bouquet of white roses in her hands. He wore jeans, a white guayabera, and sandal-style huaraches. Behind them a musical band was playing the ringing tones of "Flor de naranjo naxo loxa."

"Stevenson, take our photo." Barbara waved at him with her bouquet of flowers.

"The test of whether reincarnation exists is whether you and I find each other after living other lives," she said, walking to the market. "The last time we saw each other, I embraced you with tears in my eyes. And you gave me your hand. Our faces went dark, and everything turned to black."

"You have a good memory. Beyond unconscious time, you shine like a fruit in season," he said.

"I remember that we were on a street in ruins, like in Delos."

"You were breathing deeply, your light eyes fixed on my dark face."

"'Are you OK?' I asked you."

"That ancient love has returned. My mind is waking up; I'm beginning to perceive the memories."

"My phobias that have survived the ages have coupled with yours."

It rained. They walked, their feet covered in mud. He sheltered her with an umbrella. They entered the market to celebrate their wedding with a feast. Skinned pigs hung from hooks. They headed to doña Anita's corner stall, where the large table was covered with a plastic tablecloth and adorned with sunflowers. Howard, Guadalupe, Gabriel, Ivanna, Gerhart, Vera, and a pair of unidentified healers were seated there.

Howard and Guadalupe had arranged the menu: a plate of *Tjain T'xua,* white mushrooms in the style of María Sabina, a *tezmole* spicy with onions, *pilte de pollo* (wrapped in banana leaves and steamed) with dried chiles wrapped in *hoja santa* leaves, tlayuda-style tortillas, flavored atoles, and aguardiente made from sugarcane.

They had just started to eat when a man appeared in the passageway wearing large glasses and a huge black beard. It was Allen Ginsberg.

"Peace and love at the Gathering of Tribes for the Human Be-in."

"Welcome to the wedding," Philip greeted him.

"My companions on this journey: we are, have been, and will be ghostly travelers on an express train that we saw pass the dizzy heights of Mount Fuji and the volcano Popocatépetl, retaining only a few images in our memories. We remove the mask of our own vulnerability; we forget about the corpses on funeral pyres in India and the enraged specters on the subway in New York. Let's enter the ecstatic experiences of the ancient visions that allow us to see gods on the edges of buildings and in dark tunnels. I only want to be a heart that wishes to live right now." Ginsberg sat himself down between Philip and Barbara.

The waiters brought rice and beans to the table, cooked corn, tamales, chicken in black mole and chicken in green chile, the head of a pig crowned with garlands of cilantro and garlic, more pulque, beer, and various other alcohols.

"Who is the chick?" asked Ginsberg.

"Me," Guadalupe introduced herself.

"This chicken is my girlfriend," stuttered Howard. "She wears jeans and lets her breasts hang free under a red bandana, smokes marijuana and likes to wear pale makeup, appears buck naked like a seal in the hotel room, and at midnight she drinks espresso. Also, she aspires to be famous, like Elsa Lanchester in *The Bride of Frankenstein*."

"There are people that believe that the Beat generation was born with Ginsberg, Kerouac, and those Angry Young Englishmen," said Gabriel. "Even though the empire of the Lord of Light* believes in the beatnik, whose birth was like the birth of Frankenstein, a monster who lives on after his death."

"Why isn't the girl eating?" asked Ginsberg of Teresita de Jesús.

"Because she's shy."

"I think it's because she's just a virgin and on her period." Doña Anita sucked on her cigar and then exhaled a puff over the pots.

"I'd love to make love to her," said the teacher Herlinda. "I like the shy ones with fresh little mouths."

"Be quiet, muse of mine, I'll give you something to suck on." Gabriel raised his head off Ivanna's shoulder. But this only brought him closer to her breasts. Meanwhile the Mazatec trio of musicians sang:

¡Ay! Sandunga, Sandunga mamá, por Dios
Sandunga, no seas ingrata
Mamá de mi corazón

Suddenly Ginsberg exploded into one long "*Holy! Holy! Holy! Holy! Holy! Holy! Holy! Holy! Holy! Holy! Holy! Holy! Holy! Holy! Holy!* I've traveled from New York to Huautla to attend the wedding of Philip. I've come for one day. At nightfall I'll take a bus to old Tenochtitlán,

*This is a reference to Henry Luce, the publisher of *LIFE Magazine*.

and from there I'll go by plane to New York." With a sunflower in his hand, he recited a mantra:

> Everything is holy! Everybody's holy! Everywhere is holy! Everyday is in eternity! Everyman's an angel!
> Holy Philip holy Allen holy Barbara holy Kerouac holy Ferlinghetti holy Jasón holy Guadalupe holy Howard holy river holy mountain holy unknown holy hateful human angels holy María Sabina!

Philip then read his poem "Ceylonese Tea Candor (Pyramid Scene)":

north of
Mexico City
once called Ten
och tit lan built one
thousand ad by the Toltecs
after destruction of Teotihuacan
city of the gods . and conquered by
witch/driven Aztecs, bloody blackmagic
nazi/moloch worshipping sun devils of old
mexico who took the remains of Toltec High
Religion and turned it into degenerate center of Hell's
cult of bloody hearts torn open for the pleasure of all the
demons of the seven circles of the seven thousand webs of the
seven million fallen angels of God's solar paradise

Howard stood on a chair. For a long time he had the habit of greeting someone by holding on to their hand while smiling fixedly. He shared:

I'm going crazy, OK, but
Before you kill me or
Lock me up, I want to tell you
Something of my
Vision. I am not

Religious—believe me—I
Love women and coffee
A day in the park. I
Went walking and
Saw
The Virgin
That was all
But it has ruined me.

Lawrence Ferlinghetti interrupted: "I'm tired from the long journey from San Francisco. Tomorrow I'll leave light on the luggage / with barely any luggage, the same way I came / just as I arrived." He took a book out of his pocket. "I would like to read you *Pictures of the Gone World*":

crazy
to be alive in such a strange
world.

Gabriel Jasón interrupted, "From Malcolm Lowry I will read 'Delirium in Vera Cruz':

Where has the tenderness gone, he asked the mirror
Of the Biltmore Hotel, cuarto 216. Alas,
Can its reflection lean against the glass
Too, wondering where I have gone, into what horror?
Is that it staring at me now with terror
Behind your frail, tilted barrier? Tenderness
Was here, in this very retreat, in this
Place, its form seen, cries heard by you. What error
Is here? Am I that rashed image?
Is this the ghost of love which you reflected?
Now with a background of tequila, stubs, dirty collars,
Sodium perborate, and a scrawled page

To the dead, telephone off the hook? In rage
He smashed all the glass in the room."
(Bill: $50)

"We're leaving for our water moon," said Philip, and the pair stood up from the table.

"Many thanks, as always." Barbara bid goodbye to doña Anita.

"Before you leave, let me give you a piece of advice," said the corner restaurateur. "Don't overthink it."

Upon seeing that they were headed to the fields under the downpour, Stevenson followed them, camera in hand, taking photos. In the street they met up with a band of musicians of wind instruments (trombone, trumpet, and saxophone) once again playing "Flor de naranjo."

"William Blake protested against the nationality that Newton imposed on light," declared Philip. "I declare that light is the best distributed substance on earth."

"A flock of donkeys," exclaimed Barbara. "Seven asses of different sizes and markings climb the same steep street in step—what a sight."

"Keep moving, keep moving, let's go, let's go, we need to get to Boss Popoluca before the sun rises." A Tehuana woman wearing an embroidered huipil and a chain of golden coins spurred the donkeys on up the staircase.

"I am a believer in the Womb of the New Vision and vice president of the Black Memory Club that Proceeds the Pyramid of the New Consciousness," Philip declared. "As a wedding present I will take my beloved on a walk through a field of sunflowers." Philip stopped at the edge of a precipice and watched the sun sink behind Cerro de la Adoración.

37

VISIONS

"Welcome to the newlyweds," Ivanna greeted Philip and Barbara.

Richard Stevenson woke from a dream brought on by the landslide angel. He was stretched out on a mat, his head resting against the straw wall. The ceiling was a roof of cane leaves, and all around him mosquitos zoomed, frogs croaked. To his right were Howard and Guadalupe. Completely absorbed in themselves, they didn't look at him. A woman with breasts like floats and thighs like fishes asked the man with the flashes to take her portrait.

María Sabina, with a feverish look to her face and her eyes in a trance, sang and clapped as if her mouth and her hands moved of their own volition:

> I am the woman who knows how to swim
> I am the woman who knows how to swim in the sacred
> Because I can swim through the sea
> Because I can swim through myself

"In this mountain range, even the rain is green," Ivanna told Gabriel, as if she was dreaming of something else.

"What rain do you refer to?" he asked.

"The rain of all the days." Her fingers crawling through the shadows grabbed his hand.

"Who is that man?" he asked thickly, as if he was tripping.

"A friend, a Chilean poet, an expert in trances," Ivanna responded.

"Where is Stevenson?" asked Gordon.

"He just went out to water the plants," said Apolonia.

"And them, who are they?"

"Philip and Barbara, Howard and Guadalupe."

"Do they speak English?"

"Yes," Stevenson said, returning.

"What is your profession?" Gordon asked Gabriel Jasón.

"I am working on a cartography of the sacred places of different ethnic groups; I want to map the caves, hills, and arroyos where I've walked and listened and where I've recognized shadows and voices. This mapping has become my obsession. During my stay here I hear things that I've never seen before, I see faces that I've never heard, because things and faces, like mushrooms, have their own voices. We only need to ingest them within ourselves to hear them and know that we are listening to ourselves."

"What are the results of your search? Some investigators have been lost experimenting with the plants of the gods."

"Maria Sabina says," the teacher Herlinda began to translate for the shaman into Spanish, "'What am I doing as a spiritual woman? Seeing the world through a window and opening the doors of the imperceivable with a secret key? The more I disappear, the more I am found; the more I lose myself in the dark, the more visible I am when I return. The green mist speaks in the night, the dawn strips the black village, the hummingbirds trace aerial geometries, and the Holy Spirit, the air, is the great invisible.'"

In the room, María Sabina clapped. The mycologists and foragers followed her with their eyes as if she was a woman dreaming. Her hands spoke: her fingers looked like winged voices.

"I see, far away from here, a turquoise sun opening paths into the mountains, while a strange rain shot with supernatural rays gleams in my head. To read the signs of the rain, first one must read the metaphor of the metaphor of the metaphor of the leaves on the trees, the ones that reveal the nature of Nature," said Roger Hofmann.

"I would like to see something like that, but I just remain in the shadows of the extrasensorial," said Gordon.

"María Sabina says: 'Watch the saint of the saint dance on the border of the abyss of himself,'" Herlinda translated.

"In the Christian cult, a strange force seizes the soul when the words 'santo, santo, santo' erupt," Hofmann affirmed.

María Sabina, as if the mushrooms were speaking across her, dancing in the darkness, sang:

I am the woman who gives birth to light
I am the daughter of the woman who gives birth to light
I am the daughter of the daughter of the woman who gives birth to light
I am the daughter of the daughter of the daughter of the woman who gives birth to light
My progeny is infinite

38

FALL IN LOVE WITH HUAUTLA

LISTEN TO RADIO ORANGE BLOSSOM. WEAR HUIPILES AND TRADITIONAL CLOTHING. ATTEND THE FESTIVAL OF SAN JUAN EVANGELISTA ON DECEMBER 17TH.

Stretched from one wall to another, a cloth banner welcomed the tourists and promised visitors a menu of turkey, chickens, goats, and grasshoppers.

"Look at that gray hawk circling the mountain. Dark brown eyes, vanilla yellow thighs, it hasn't stopped staring at me." Barbara, standing with her legs spread on a rock, tried to maintain her balance.

"I like the vultures better, most of all their black feathers and their red heads," said Philip.

"I'm Rosalindo Flores, the local teacher in the rural primary school Benemérito de las Américas. I'm also the first assistant teacher to Herlinda Martínez, in compliance with the organization. I usually assist Miss Pike with her evangelical work throughout the Sierra Mazateca," she said behind them, as if she had been listening to them.

"What do you want?"

"I wanted to alert you. The Son of Dolores is coming here, a predator who has a vulture as his nagual. He doesn't have a name of his own, he's just known that way."

"Why do you need to alert us?"

"Well, not because of the minor crimes he commits in the market, like stealing meat from the butchers, stealing chickens, pigs, eggs, but because of what he's plotting. I don't want him to hear us talking—he's malicious, and he carries a folding knife and a machete, and he attacks people in deserted areas. He also runs with other evildoers."

"Who are they?"

"Good-for-nothings from the neighboring towns who will kill someone over a mere look or touch. They go around in stolen clothes and trashed shoes, kidnap girls from the school and bring them back deflowered. Another time they left a chicken with its throat cut in teacher Herlinda's classroom. If you've seen him, watch out, because you'll keep seeing him."

"Vulture," exclaimed Philip.

"Brother vulture with his head painted in yellows and grays performs a socially beneficial work. He cleans the fields and the ravines of carrion," explained Rosalindo Flores, Bible in hand. "I wish there were spiritual vultures that could clean the internal carrion from the neighbors, those pigs and whores, who would pull out the fingernails of the policemen and politicians. That's why I care more for my baldies with red heads and plucked bodies than for human beings. Can I help with anything? Can I recommend some local arts and crafts in the market? Do you want to buy huaraches, huipiles, pants, homespun shirts? Or would you rather have a tour of the town and its surroundings? Would you like to visit the Río Santiago, the cemetery, the cave of Cerro Rabón?

"Another time." Philip and Barbara said goodbye and walked away.

Just then an old man appeared on the trail. Philip noticed that he carried a cardboard box with holes punched in it, as if for an animal to breathe through. In the distance a bolt of lightning flashed. From the box he heard the sounds of wings beating, a high-pitched hissing, and the drumming of feathered talons. The old man opened the lid and brought out an eagle. Its neck turned so far toward Philip, it appeared to be twisted; its yellow claws were clutching a rattlesnake. The last rays of the setting sun illuminated its eyes. The eagle resembled a fallen angel.

"I'm selling an eagle," said the old man.

"I'll pay you, but I won't buy it," replied Philip.

"I don't understand."

"Twenty dollars."

"One hundred. We trapped it on the Cerro de la Adoración."

"Fifty." Philip proceeded to free the eagle right in front of the bewildered eyes of the man. In a flash, it flew over his head and away.

39

GORDON AND TATIANA

At dusk, Nicholas Gordon, wearing a plaid shirt and jeans, declared: "I'm leaving, setting off for the Mapimí Silent Zone. I've had a vision of God among the cacti."

"Where is that?" Tatiana emerged onto the path.

"In the Bolsón of Mapimí. During the velada I saw an adobe wall and some saguaro spines and a floating book with painted stones, *The Book of Images.*"

"Why would you want to live among the blue agaves and creeping nopales? Do you really think you will find God in the desert surrounded by spiny plants?"

"The sacred cacti will show us the way to invisible thresholds. There's so much life in them, in their flesh and spines, and life in the silence they grow with their green fingers pointing at the sky."

"Well, if you say so, then your woman goes with you."

"Let me think about it."

"I've already decided."

"OK, but keep that hurtful look that wounds my feelings with poisonous darts away from me."

"Are you really ready to leave this place, now that you've just begun to understand the properties of the mushrooms?"

"Over time I've noticed that each one takes the dosage that they deserve. Some people require more mushrooms to intensify their visions and prolong their effect; the dose doesn't increase with usage. In others, the mushrooms sharpen their memory while destroying their sense of time."

"It's seemed to me that we've only been here a few seconds."

"I feel like it's been years, that in the space of one velada, we've lived eons."

"Your pupils look dilated, and your pulse is weak."

"We've been searching more than thirty years for the magic mushroom, just to now leave so soon."

"We'll return."

"Are you sure?"

"I'll tell you later what I've discovered. Right now my head hurts, maybe because of stress, or maybe because of the cumulative effect of all the mushrooms I've taken during our stay here."

"If your head hurts, I have analgesics. If you're nauseous because of the mushrooms, I have pills for indigestion."

"You're a walking pharmacy, but I'm having a hard time breathing; my right leg is hurting." He undid the laces of his boot and discovered his foot was bristling with a bouquet of cactus spines.

"I'll tell María Sabina to cure you by putting an egg on your forehead."

"Let's rest for now. At dawn we leave for the Zone of Silence."

"Hey, Crescencio García, tell me, the path for your feet, the path for your footprints, and the path of your forgetting, where do they lead?" María Sabina suddenly interjected while smoking a fat cigar.

"Hey, Lady Singsong, sip, sip, sip, hummingbird, work, work, rain, rain," responded her Mazatec friend, half his body in shadow.

Gordon and Tatiana passed by Philip without greeting him; they didn't want to say goodbye to anyone. Upon opening the door, they felt the dawn air on their faces.

Richard Stevenson photographed them walking through the cornfields, loaded down with bags of *Psilocybe mexicana* for their travels. Outside the hut, by the light of the moon, two girls were tripping in a trance, barefoot, holding hands, turning and turning in circles, dying of laughter, until finally they fell on the ground, exhausted. Above, completely oblivious to them, bats headed straight toward the cave of the lords of the hills, of the rivers, and of the springs. When they got to the great oak, Stevenson saw Gordon and Tatiana change their minds and return to María Sabina's house.

"Good morning," they said as they sat down on the mats and listened to the singing of the shaman.

"I like music. The Principal Beings, when they showed me the book, told me that they loved images. They told me that they wanted to dance with me. One Principal Being was my partner. With him I danced to "Flor de naranjo" in a vision while I told him of my problems: that they had burned my house down, that I had been robbed of what little I owned, that two bullets had entered my body when they wanted to kill me, and that when I lost my teeth I was ashamed of my toothlessness. He, still dancing, told me not to worry, that he was in love with me, with me, the Principal Clown."

I am the woman drummer
I am the woman trumpeter
I am the woman violinist
I am the musical woman

40

BEATNIKS AND MYCOLOGISTS

Ivanna brought Gabriel to the velada on Thursday, as previously arranged with María Sabina. Gabriel brought Philip. And Philip brought Barbara, Howard, and Guadalupe. At the entrance of the shack, leaning on the adobe wall, was a man with long hair, wearing a suit of handwoven cloth and huaraches, playing a handmade violin. Next to him, a girl tripping with enraptured eyes reveled in the music.

The beatnik contingent arrived before the mycologists because they wanted to watch the shaman prepare the altar, place her saints on the table, and choose the mushrooms for the velada while performing ritual cleansing.

"There are no mirrors here," Ivanna complained as she looked through the rooms for a place to do her hair.

"Our interior face is only known by the Principal Beings," said María Sabina.

"Why would you want to become attached to a face that will become wrinkled, that ruptures like the skin of a drum and ages until it loses all resemblance to the face of childhood?" Tatiana muttered.

"Do you have a new dog?" asked Barbara.

"It's a stray dog. It came from the hill. The problem with dogs is that eventually they die," María Sabina said to her.

"Come in." Apolonia stood at the door and received the visitors.

"Thank you." The beatniks didn't need an invitation to make themselves at home; they entered and spread out on the seats and sleeping mats.

"Coffee?" said Barbara, offering to prepare it.

"Where is Howard?" Guadalupe looked for him among those present.

"He's off looking for the Eye of God," Gabriel said while holding Ivanna's hand.

"I just saw the sun looking down toward the earth. They say that the rays of its crown represent the celestial origins of the American Indians," Howard affirmed from the doorway.

"Who invited the members of the disgraceful beatnik scene to come here?" asked Stevenson.

"I invited them, and María Sabina agreed," replied Ivanna.

"Everyone has their visions. I have my own, you have yours, and all of us respect the madness of the other," said Guadalupe.

"If it's not a bother, please remain silent," Gordon requested.

"I hope that you have been abstinent from sexual acts before attending the rite. If someone hasn't done so, they can excuse themselves now," Roger scrutinized the participants.

"We're clean," Gabriel Jasón assured him. "The velada may begin. If anyone wants to leave, they should do so now and not bother the rest of us."

"The use of hallucinogenic mushrooms is a ritual practice passed down from pre-Hispanic times. This ceremony is a survivor of a world of magic." Gordon ate the mushrooms that María Sabina handed him after smoking them over the copal.

"Consecrated. The God Meat." Gabriel Jasón ate them as if he was ingesting a sacred wafer.

"Where am I?" asked Barbara from the shadows.

"In the center of the earth," María Sabina responded.

"And to my right?"

"The center of the earth."

"To my left?"

"The center of the earth."

"And those mountains, those caves, those arroyos, those cities, those cliffs. Where are they?"

"In the center of the earth."

"And that which we don't see?"

"The center of the earth."

"And us, what are we?"

"Children of the center of the earth." María Sabina, as if the mushroom spoke using her body, began to dance and clap. She offered a song:

I am the woman who births
I am the daughter of the woman who births
I am the daughter of the daughter of the daughter of the woman who births
My progeny is infinite

"What's wrong?" Gordon drew near to her when he saw that she had stopped, paralyzed, in the middle of her song.

"I have a premonition that something bad is about to happen."

"What are you worried about?"

"In the coming days, the Son of Dolores will become known as the killer of Cerro Central. After hiding out for months in the mountains, he will become known as the dismemberer of Cerro Central. He will kill his woman and daughter by hacking them up. The municipal police will arrest him. His neighbors in the Cerro Central will denounce him. Using the false name of Juan Manuel Gómez Robles, he will attempt to kill a muleteer with an axe. He, completely possessed, will be tied up, and he will ask, yelling, to be freed so that he can kill three more people. Upon making an inspection of his home, the authorities will uncover a decapitated girl next to her mother, whose skull will have been broken into pieces. Both, having disappeared a few weeks before, will be found like offerings on an altar of skulls in Cerro Central."

41

MURDER

"There will be a man in the room. A face camouflaged by darkness. This unknown man will leave the door open. The altar will be empty of mushrooms." María Sabina watched an intruder leaning against the wall. "There will be two men in coats. Behind them will be an ox with red eyes, a toad with sad eyes, and a little one who is neither a girl or a dwarf will appear. Holy Mother, am I dreaming while awake? Do I see my son stabbed? Santo, santo, santo, make it so I don't believe in them because they don't exist."

"I'm going to see what's happening." Stevenson heard mosquitos buzzing. Outside of the house he heard the sound of someone coughing. The cold was rising. The walls were marked with the numbers one, three, six. On the stone upon which María Sabina sat to look down at the town, someone had spilled red paint.

"María Sabina," chided an unknown man with wiry hair and beady black eyes like black widow spiders.

"Who are you?"

"The Son of Dolores."

"What's your name?" asked Gordon.

"I don't have a name of my own."

"And who is this Dolores?"

"The mother of betrayals," a third man entered and said.

The first had yellow teeth, as if he had spent the day gnawing on corncobs.

"The señora wants you to leave." Gordon stood in front of the three of them.

"No, míster, we would rather stay." The Son of Dolores tested the edge of his knife with his thumb. Another man hung back to his side. His eyeless face was divided into two halves by a knife held between his teeth.

"It does no good to ask them to leave." Apolonia sighed.

"It's one in the morning, and the cold's claws are scratching at the windowpanes. Something is going to happen," said Philip.

The Son of Dolores advanced upon María Sabina with the knife. Gordon made a movement to stop him, while she hurled smoldering copal at him.

"We'll be back." The dark figure hid the knife under his shirt. As he faded away, he left behind the smell of wet wool and burnt flesh.

"Yes, there are mirrors." Ivanna looked at her reflection in the pane of the window.

"I can't stand blisters on my feet," griped Gabriel Jasón.

"Mother, don't worry, soon we'll reach the shore of the night and be safe." Aurelio was completely gone; he seemed sick or perhaps even mentally disturbed.

"If my eyes aren't lying, we need more light." Apolonia changed the spent candles and lit new ones.

"I know what is going to happen as if it had already happened, and I began to forget when it still hasn't happened. Everything lived is forgettable by nature." María Sabina crossed the room as if shaken by the impact of her vision. And as if the mushrooms were speaking with her mouth, she uttered something before the invisible figure standing next to her son.

"I don't understand why you address your son as if he was dead." Stevenson filmed and photographed. "I hope you will begin to dance."

"I don't have the will to tonight."

"María Sabina says that the man with the hazy face watching her from the stairs disturbs her greatly. She knows he doesn't exist, but how she wishes he would leave," said the teacher Herlinda.

"The Son of Dolores left?" the voice of Apolonia asked incredulously as the flames of the candles went out. "I'll light them again." She drew close to each one. She tossed coffee beans and maize on the floor. The girl on mushrooms who was with the violinist began to sob, weighed down by the torrent of visions that was pouring out of her eyes.

"Mamá says that Aurelio is sad because he knows they will kill him. 'Mamá, I know that I will be lost,' he doesn't stop repeating," said Apolonia. "Mamá knows that something terrible is coming. Mamá asks that you hang a basket of mushrooms from the roof and that you shut both doors to the fields so that the Son of Dolores doesn't come in. Mamá says that the fresh mushrooms, normally the color of green straw and dark roasted coffee, have turned blue, brown, and black because of the tragedy that approaches."

"With this one it will be five that I've killed." The Son of Dolores reappeared in the room dragging a rotten hide.

"Did you hear what he said?" asked María Sabina.

"Yes, I heard. He's the murderer," Apolonia reassured her.

"Why does he want to kill? Is there a motive?" asked Herlinda.

"Aurelio was a salesman, and the Son of Dolores owed him fifty pesos. That's why he killed him," Apolonia confirmed, as if the crime had already been committed. "María Sabina says that when they stab Aurelio they should wrap his head in a huipil with flowers embroidered by her hand so that his black hair stays fresh under the new moon."

"They killed my son!" exclaimed María Sabina in Spanish, her eyes bulging out at the premonition.

"It's me, it's me. With this it will be five that I've murdered," a cowskin yelled from the floor, a rotting hide with the features of the Son of Dolores.

"Mamá, did you hear what it said?" asked Apolonia.

"Yes, I saw it, heard it, it belongs to Dolores, he's come to the store to drink aguardiente," she answered. "Three men have come. The Son of Dolores will ask about Aurelio, and I will tell him that he is playing the guitar in another room. I will invite him in. My son will offer him a drink. Drunk, they will start to sing. Suddenly the Son of Dolores will insult him, he will pull up his shirt, and he will take out the knife. He will lunge at him like an angry bull and stick him in the throat. Aurelio falls next to the door that leads to the store. Herlinda tries to bandage his throat. In the place where the Son of Dolores was, all that will remain is a cowhide. The murderer will take off running, a knife in hand. With his accomplices he will flee to San Miguel." María Sabina seemed disturbed by the premonition. The last candle went out, and darkness invaded the room. She fell to the floor.

Outside the house, they heard the sounds of bare feet running through the cornfields, rifle shots, people yelling: "Murder! Murder!"

42

MURDERERS ON THE RUN

No one dared to detain the fugitives. The people, believing that they were the walking dead fleeing the approaching dawn, avoided them completely.

The mycologists, foragers, and beatniks, still sluggish from of the effects of the Holy Children, all left together, exhaustedly crossing the cornfields. They hadn't made it even twenty meters when they ran into the Son of Dolores. They noticed his thigh, green as the rib of a maguey whitened by the dew. Just for a moment, though, because he immediately leaped out of the way and was lost among the coffee plants.

His accomplices followed frantically, as if no matter where they hid, they would be found by the Holy Children. They never stopped looking back, afraid that the invisible spirit of María Sabina was following them. It wasn't enough to just escape to a ravine or ditch; passing through rocks and undergrowth, they kept themselves hidden. Then everyone heard the sound of a motor, and all of their eyes turned to the brushwood. On the other side of the path was a convertible junker, the Son of Dolores sitting at the wheel. His accomplices were in the back.

"He can't get it running." Gabriel Jasón heard a voice coming from over near the wheezing car.

The Son of Dolores leaned out of the window and pointed an ancient pistol at the Chilean. He paused, watching him. He shook his head, and the car began to roar while belching smoke.

"The Son of Dolores is cursed by the mushroom. It doesn't matter where he hides. He will die." The mushroom forager Aristeo had set off walking, talking only of the slopes of the mountains he intended to ascend or descend.

The mycologists carried bags of mushrooms and coffee and a bottle of aguardiente for their thirst. When they saw Dolores sitting on a rock, teeth bared, waiting for death, this served as a signal, for some reason, to bid each other goodbye.

Stevenson, ignoring the stomach pains he was having because of ingesting some Holy Children during the velada, continued taking photos as if he was trying to use up all the rolls of film he carried in his backpack.

"I am still interested in publishing your photos in my book about the veladas," Hofmann told him. "Would you send them to me?"

"I go to the afterlife; you can contact me there." The photographer turned the camera downward so he could capture an image of the car of the Son of Dolores disappearing into the mist on Cerro del Fortín and another of the mushroom foragers ascending the stairs of the steep streets as if they were heading into the sky. From afar, the sound of an invisible rooster seemed to rip through the haze.

Tatiana, distraught over the killing of Aurelio, spoke with her husband about the episodes of violence in Huautla since their arrival, when she was surrounded by a bunch of women who protected her body from the rain with their tiny umbrellas. Guided by the mule driver Óscar Wilde Gómez, they were directed to the Cerro de la Adoración. The ascent, dishearteningly, took at least an hour. There they would see the altar with images of the Virgin Mary and Chicón Nindó or Toxoco, the lord of the hills and mountains.

"I hope that the animals released of their cargos walk easily through the fields of cane sugar," Ivanna said to Gabriel.

"Remember one pass leads to another pass leads to another pass and more passes that lead to more passes until the path ends at a cliff."

Gordon breathed the pure air of the morning while directing his gaze at the green mist that enveloped the vegetation.

"María Sabina says," translated the teacher Herlinda, "'The neighbors will come to the wake. They will drink aguardiente and play cards. I will give them coffee, bread, and cigarettes. With the money they place near the body, I will pay the cost of burial. During the night, a healer, drinking gulps of aguardiente and burning copal, will direct their invocations to the lords of the hills and the Catholic saints. They will try to return Aurelio's soul to his body and will call Aurelio by his name so as to little by little bring his spirit to the place where his master is, the dead one who lies on a mat, bathed and in clean clothes. When it is believed that he is present, his spirit will dissipate. Twenty-four hours after his death, he will be placed in a wooden casket with water, clay vessels, tortillas, a comb, and tools and coins for the journey. We will bring him to the cemetery accompanied by the ringing of the bells. A musical band will join the funeral party, playing his favorite songs. A black dog will guide his steps to the other world and will help him to cross the wide and deep river of death.'" María Sabina offered as if her voice came from the mushrooms: "For weeks and months, the soldiers, with the help of friends and relatives, will search the area. They will look for the Son of Dolores in caves and ravines, without finding his face. But the killers of Aurelio will die. The violence of bad people comes back to them. They will be killed by people who don't know them. For months, I will cry for the death of my son."

The funeral party descended Cerro del Fortín in a line stretching to the main street. Four men in homespun shirts and pants carried the casket, which was adorned with black ribbons. The mourners did not weep; they recited Ave Marías. María Sabina paid no attention to them. Dressed in her best huipil, shoeless, her face as wrinkled as a prune, she walked on, chewing a cigar in her toothless mouth.

"The mushroom helped me in my journeys to see the stars; now it will help me to walk the paths of a sky extinguished by death." She crossed the shadows of the cemetery.

Philip looked at the graveyard circled by mountains. The priest repeated religious dogma that emerged in Latin, Spanish, and Mazatec.

Barbara wore tight black pants that she had bought in a store that catered to Indigenous women. Her butt and thigh were clearly visible through a large tear.

"Lord take pity on your son Aurelio, receive him in your holy kingdom." The priest sprinkled holy water over the casket; the gravedigger, shovelfuls of wet dirt.

"How old was he? Nineteen, twenty?" asked Tatiana, looking somber. Under her eyes, dark shadows were visible through her makeup.

"It's time to be thinking of María Sabina; she seems fragile and vulnerable." Gordon held her by her arm and, accompanied by Tatiana, Stevenson, and Hofmann, set off on the way back to the shaman's house.

"We're staying," Gabriel said to Ivanna while watching a priest head off with an acolyte as young as a masturbating boy.

"Us also." Guadalupe started to walk next to Howard.

"The children's earth tombs, the clay tombstones of the mayors, the glassy gravestones, the pots of flowers, even death itself, it's all new," added Philip.

"The sun isn't bothered by the heat of noon." Barbara watched the mycologists standing among the grasses and quadrupeds. Her hair was so luminous it was almost transparent.

43

FEDERALES

"At that time, some people came who spoke Castilian and dressed like people from the city. A Mazatec interpreter came with them," María Sabina recounted later in her life story, *Vida de María Sabina, la sabia de los hongos*.

"They entered my house, without me asking them to enter. They fixed their eyes on some Holy Children that I had out on a little table. One of them pointed at them and asked: 'If I asked you for mushrooms, would you give those to me?'

"'Yes, because I believe you've come in search of God,' I told him. Another one of them ordered me with an authoritative voice: 'Come with us to San Andrés Hidalgo. We're searching for a person who, like you, is determined to make people crazy.'

"Meanwhile, the other people in the group searched my entire house. One of them showed the rest a bottle that contained San Pedro. He told them solemnly: 'This is tobacco mixed with the mineral lime and garlic. It protects against bad spirits.'

"'You smoke it?' One of the men asked in a booming voice.

"'No,' I responded, 'This is a type of tobacco that you rub on the arms of the sick and also pour a little in the mouth . . .'

"Another person carried papers about me in his hands. He showed the others the records and the record player that Wasson had given me. All of them turned to look at me, and he said I couldn't speak Castilian with them, but they could see in these papers what I was. . . . Later with some delicacy they put me in a truck, and I obeyed without resistance. I sat between a man driving and another who sat next to the door. The one next to the door kept eyeing the papers where my image appeared. I noticed that every once in a while, he looked at me from the corner of his eye.

"At no time did I feel terror, though I understood that these people were the authorities and were trying to harm me. We arrived at San Andrés, and there they arrested the local agent. Finally, I understood that this man and I were accused of selling a tobacco that was driving young people mad.

"Later, they took us to the municipal president. A doctor from the National Institute of Indigenous Peoples spoke with the men. They talked for a long time. In the end, the medical professional said, 'Don't worry, María Sabina, nothing will happen to you. We are here to protect you.' Also, the men who arrested me said, 'Forgive us, go home and get some rest . . .'"

While this was happening to María Sabina, four police vehicles pulled up in front of the market. Doña Anita turned upon hearing the sound of all the motors. Two uniformed policemen and three federal agents were making their way toward the establishment where Philip and Barbara were eating. A young waitress had just brought them a plate of chicken with forest mushrooms in salsa verde, warm tortillas, and coffee from Huautla. Philip was wearing dark glasses to protect his sensitive eyes.

"Your pants are ripped, you slept on the ground," Barbara told him. She was dressed in a huipil with two knotted ribbons as a belt. Her flaming red hair was loose. Her big feet with their uncared-for nails spilled out of her sandals.

"May I?" A federal agent with gold teeth and raccoon-like aviator glasses proceeded to inspect them while his commander pointed a gun at Philip. "You're under arrest."

"I don't want any problems." Philip stood up from the table with his hands raised.

"He has marijuana." A policeman removed a few filthy cigarettes from the pockets of his pants.

"You too, señora." The federal agent ran his hands over Barbara's body. In his search, he felt her breasts, her butt, and her abdomen and squeezed her thighs. "Give me your bag. Yes, there's grass in here. You're under arrest, cutie."

"Come with us, please." The commander and the other policemen restrained them in view of the salespeople and the shoppers in the market and directed them to the rundown local police cars.

Keeping their guns trained on Philip, they removed his glasses, tied his hands together, and took him to a police vehicle out front.

"What are you hiding here?" The police who had accosted them in the barbershop walked over and twisted Philip's nipples under his shirt.

"A poem."

"I'm going to beat a poem into your head." The police hit him with a club and removed a notebook from his bag, looking for proof of drug dealing. Without finding anything compromising, he unbuttoned his shirt and ran his hands over his naked chest. Bringing his face close to Philip's, he examined him with vicious eyes: "Anything to declare?"

"On my face I declare some wrinkles, a stubble beard, and some premature gray hairs; the rest is internal," said Philip in halting Spanish.

Just then, Apolonia appeared with a jar of honey containing six pairs of Holy Children mushrooms.

"María Sabina sent them to you so you can keep searching for the holy," she told them. But one of the federal agents slapped her hand away, and the jar fell to the floor.

"You've looked over the woman? Her tits, her ass, her thighs?" The commander pointed to Barbara. "Get her into the convertible Jeep. We'll put them in separate cells in DF."

"I'll look for you in San Francisco," she yelled.

"The nightmare is beginning," he said. "Maybe we won't see each other again. You find the constellations, and I'll meet up with Mercury; each of us will be married to the universe."

"Philip!" she yelled as they took her away, her red hair floating in the air like a Persephone of the plains being abducted, not by Hades, but by devils of the underworld.

"Barbara," called Philip. But he no longer saw her; he could only see the hairy chauffeur who seemed to have sprouted wings from his ears.

"We'll come back later for the other fuckers and clean all the unwanted foreigners out of this town. The army will rid the place of the degenerates shortly. Though with the military come reporters, medics, and meddlers. We'll request the government not allow any beatniks to enter until we say," stated the commander.

"Look at this pothead with red eyes and burning hair—she looks like she's burning up from the inside," muttered a federal agent.

"Are you going to deport me?" asked Gerhart Münch.

"The sloshed musician? No, him no. For what?" The commander stamped out a Delicados cigarette butt.

"And me?" asked Vera.

"No, señora, you are a resident."

Howard and Guadalupe were on their way to the market, the wilderness at their backs, when they saw Philip and Barbara arrested. They ducked into a store under the pretext of buying a kilo of coffee. In order to stay out of sight, they wasted time by pretending to make a long-distance telephone call. Suddenly Teresita de Jesús appeared in a huipil embroidered all over in birds and flowers.

"I came to help you," she told them. "I heard about the operation."

Her smile cheered up Howard, who took her by the hand and looked at her kindly.

"I'm going with you. I've brought enough to pay for my trip."

"You can't come with us. The police are looking for us. And we don't know where we're going from here. Take these and think of us." Guadalupe took off her earrings and gave them to her.

"I can't take these."

"Take them, that's an order."

"You haven't even left, and I already miss you," Teresita looked at the couple nostalgically, as if they were already gone. "Take care of yourselves."

"One step further into the abyss, though we haven't hit bottom yet," joked Guadalupe.

"Take this for the trip." She gave them a wrapped packet of landslide mushrooms and a bag of oranges.

Without turning back to look at her again, they headed to the Hotel Grande to let the others know about the raid. But they were informed by Casimira in reception that some federal agents had come looking for them, and so they fled immediately to the bus station. There, in one of the most public places in town, sitting on a wooden bench, they wrapped themselves in serapes and pretended to be sleeping so as to evade notice. They left on the first bus of the day.

As he later told the teacher Herlinda, Gabriel Jasón passed the afternoon in a cantina on the edge of town scrounging for glasses of aguardiente that he didn't drink and spicy tacos that he didn't eat. Completely sober, he crossed the street and went down to the plaza to a newsstand, where he bought the book *The Mazatecs and the Indigenous Problem in Cuenca del Papaloapan*. The book was an awkward size to carry hidden, so he put it in a string bag, which he then forgot on the counter.

While he was waiting in the street for Ivanna, Gabriel saw Popoluca pass by with his women, makeup smeared on their faces: Rosa Quetzal, Tomasa the Tehuana, Juana the Mixe, and Teresa the Tzeltal, with her daughter of the huge almond eyes. The pimp, with his typical white pants, patent leather shoes, and colored vest, had become friendly with the local officials and was on the cusp of opening his club, Mambo No. 5. While Gabriel made a great show at the joy of seeing them all again, they passed by him slowly, without speaking a single word. Except the little girl, that is, who turned to look at him with a huge smile.

When Ivanna found him, the two walked toward the plaza and ran into Powell, the speleologist, who pretended not to know them. They hid in the brushwood and only left their hiding place when night fell.

Delfina and Casimira went looking for Gabriel in the wooden room that served as a terminal waiting room, but they didn't approach when they saw he was with Ivanna. They waved at him from afar and disappeared. Ivanna said that she would go flag a taxi, and Gabriel waited for her to return seated on a trunk behind the terminal. She came back a half an hour later with a coffee in her hand and a suitcase in the other. The police were combing the streets, the market, and the plaza, but they didn't catch them. There were no taxis. She had purchased two tickets for the bus at eleven that night. She also told him that the police commander was guarding Cerro del Fortín, and he had posted a sentry in front of María Sabina's house. They had interrogated the mycologists about their whereabouts and had posted reserves to arrest them. Casimira and Delfina then returned to advise them on the movements of the police and to tell them they could board the bus at eleven. They stayed with them until it was time for Ivanna and Gabriel to leave.

Returning to the hotel, they listened to the Voice of Radio Huautla reading the news of the night:

> This morning a cow drowned in the Santiago River. Yesterday on Friday, the boy Rómulo González didn't come back to school. Teacher Herlinda is asking if anyone knows his whereabouts. Double feature this Sunday in Cineac, *Casablanca* and *Subida al cielo*. Don't miss it.
>
> Fernando Pérez, originally from Villahermosa, Tabasco, and Moisés Mastín, originally of Torreón, Coahuila, agents of the Federal Narcotics Police, report the arrest of two undesirable foreigners in the local market. They state they were carrying out their duties of service as charged along the main street, above the market in the post number 8, when, at 12:30, they saw two individuals who seemed to be foreigners sitting and smoking marijuana. For this reason, they proceeded to interrogate them, especially after these two individuals tossed the cigarette they had been smoking down the drain. After detaining them, the agents stated that they found the one named Philip carried a small red metal box like those for holding cigarettes, of the English brand Craven "A," in-

> side of which was a blue-colored paper the size of a business card that contained marijuana that was prepared for smoking. Upon seeing this, they proceeded to cite Philip, from San Francisco, California, thirty-one years of age, occupation writer, and his accomplice, who responds to the name Barbara, originally from New York, New York. The suspects, of US nationality, accredited their legal stay in the country as tourists with visas issued by the Secretaría de Gobernación for 120 days.

Philip and Barbara were transported in separate vehicles to the private prison of the Secretaría de Gobernación on calle de Miguel Schulz, number 136, Colonia San Rafael, where they were charged with committing health violations. After having their photos taken head on and in profile and after being fingerprinted, the beatniks were taken by police in plainclothes to different dormitories. They were permitted no visitors, neither Mexicans nor foreigners.

A jailer walked Philip to his cell. Before leaving him in the windowless room with dirty green walls and a carpet fit for a mangy dog, the jailer pointed to some graffiti scrawled on the wall in red marker:

THE MAN THAT WALKS THROUGH WALLS
MAKES HISTORY.

HERE, FIDEL CASTRO AND ERNESTO GUEVARA
DREAMED OF THE REVOLUTION AND THE DIRTY RAT
WHO PUT THEM IN JAIL.

"You have the good luck of occupying one of the best cells in this migrant prison. This is the place where last year for one month the guerilla fighters Fidel Castro and Ernesto Guevara were held. If you are interested, for one hundred pesos I will sell you a copy of the investigation papers about the conspiracy against the government of the Republic of Cuba that was written by Captain Fernando Gutiérrez Barrios, chief of controls for the Federal Security Directorate."

"Yes, I'm interested!"

"I'll come back later," said the jailer, and as promised he returned a few hours later with a file of papers that he placed on the cot. "Don't open them now, look at them when you are alone. It's a lot to take in."

When he left, Philip began to read the report of the fearsome Fernando Gutiérrez Barrios, who carried out the investigation and arrest of the conspirators.

> On the 21st day of June of 1956, we followed a Packard vehicle, 1950 model, color green, with license plate IW55655 from Miami, Florida, that left from a house at number 49, calle Emparan, with five individuals inside. At the intersection of the streets Mariano Escobedo and Kepler, we saw three of those individuals descend in a suspicious manner with the intention of disappearing into the night, upon which we proceeded to detain them, and discovered they were armed and that they were transporting a rifle, Ceska 30.06, and 980 cartridges of the same caliber in the interior of the vehicle. The DFS agents traveled in two vehicles, one in front and another traveling behind the suspicious vehicle. When they found themselves surrounded, a tall and corpulent man, assumed to be the leader, attempted to use his firearm, but one of my agents placed his pistol on his neck, thereby impeding his movement.
>
> The arrested persons responded to the names Fidel Alejandro Castro Ruz, arrived in Mexico in July of 1955 on a DC-6 bimotored plane on a commercial "lechero" flight*, that made stops in Mérida and in Veracruz, from where he traveled to DF by bus. The other four detainees, Ciro Redondo García, Universo Sánchez Álvarez, Ramiro Valdez Menéndez and Reynaldo Benitez Nápoles, revealed themselves to be Cuban nationals and political exiles. None of them presented documentation, they stated that had been hiding out in the residence at 49 Emparan, belonging to one María Antonia González, where they had met Fidel Castro and Ernesto Guevara. Arrested because of this inves-

*This is a reference to the small planes that serviced rural farms delivering and transporting goods.

tigation, we then established a watch over the aforementioned house at 49 Emparan, where the same day at 1400 hours, 22 additional Cuban conspirators were arrested. The DFS confiscated false passports, firearms, among which were found .38 caliber Star machine guns, a Mauser Waffenfabrik pistol, hand grenades of US origin, special charges, and boxes of bullets. The direction of all these arms was controlled by Castro Ruz, who received correspondence from his loyalists through one Sra. Hilda Gadea de Guevara, Peruvian political exile, married to one Ernesto Guevara de la Serna, Argentinian national, with whom she had one daughter. Guevara de la Serna was the personal chief of staff for, and active member in the band of, Fidel Alejandro Castro Ruz.

These two traveled to the cities of Toluca and Cuernavaca and went to the movies to see *Arriba el telón* starring Cantiflas. The aforementioned Guevara was asthmatic and poor and had a post at the Hospital General in the allergy department, where he undertook experiments with stray cats he captured in nearby neighborhoods. In his free time, he worked as a street photographer with a Retina 35mm camera. During his detention he showed himself to be defiant and declared himself a Marxist-Leninist.

During the interrogation of the persons detailed, it was discovered that Cuban political exiles residing in this country had formed a group called "26 de Julio," run by Fidel Alejandro Castro Ruz with the objective of overthrowing the acting Cuban government in the following six or seven weeks, and that according to them, they were assured of the support of 90% of the population of their country, and that owing to political differences with the government, this Cuban population had received over the past few years a huge number of arms, which they had hidden waiting for a favorable moment. This group used the name "26 de Julio" because on that date in 1953, they rallied an armed insurrection against the General Fulgencio Batista and stormed the Moncada Barracks under the leadership of Castro Ruz.

With the intention of military preparation, the aforementioned individuals held practices in Rancho Santa Rosa, in the Chalco region, where they trained members of the Che Guevara's band, and whose instructors included also Castro Ruz, Sr., Alberto Bayo Giroud, a Cuban national who was a colonel in the Spanish Civil War, and Arsacio Vanegas Arroyo, a wrestling coach, grandson of the populist printmaker, the artist José Guadalupe Posada.

In the middle of the night, after saying, "Follow me," a jailer led Philip to a windowless room with no furniture, excepting a table, chair, and sink to wash the blood off the hands of the interrogators. "I want to introduce you to Captain Fernando Gutiérrez Barrios. I should warn you that the captain detests lies, and if you cooperate this interview will be fast and painless." The jailer departed.

"What brings you here?" After a long period of silence, a man with a hard gaze and brusque manners sat down at the table across from Philip. Meanwhile another jailer continued standing just beside him.

"What are the charges?"

"I ask the questions. You answer only, 'Yes, señor' or 'No, señor.'"

"Yes, señor."

"Have you had any contact with Marxist-Leninist groups active in this country or coming out of Cuba, Guatemala, or Nicaragua?"

"No, señor."

"Is there a plan to assassinate President Eisenhower?"

"None that I am aware of, señor."

"What can you tell me about the black market that operates on the border?"

"I don't know anything about that, señor."

"What about the derelict groups that traffic morphine, heroin, cocaine, and firearms?"

"I know no such group, señor. My wife, Barbara, and I, both American nationals, have been spending time in Huautla de Jiménez, Oaxaca, without any other incidents besides our arrest."

At the end of the interrogation, Captain Gutiérrez slapped the table and took a photo from Philip that had been taken of him at his apartment in calle Oslo number 3, Colonia Juárez. "I'll keep this photo." Standing on the balcony, Philip was looking off toward calle de Niza, long-haired, wearing a plaid shirt, a borrowed jacket, and shoes of different sizes and colors, and he seemed discombobulated.

They treated Barbara a little better. She was permitted to walk outside on the patio, visit the cafeteria, look through the prison bars to the street, and speak with people passing by outside who offered to buy her cigarettes, which they then smoked holding the money in hand. After two routine interrogations without a defense lawyer, the Dirección General de Población announced that Philip would be deported through the main airport in Mexico City. The United States Embassy urged the Mexican authorities to relieve themselves of these undesirables and had intervened to have Philip taken out of the country as soon as possible.

While Philip waited for the execution of this repatriation order, his jailer came to tell him about how the Cubans Fidel Alejandro Castro Ruz and Ernesto Guevara de la Serna, alias "El Che," had been liberated on July 24 thanks to the intervention of the ex-president Lázaro Cárdenas with the acting president Adolfo Ruiz Cortines and how together, in the rain, Castro and Guevara set off the dawn of November 25 for Tuxpan, and there where the river connects with the Gulf of Mexico they set off for Cuba in a yacht called Granma.

Three days after Philip's deportation, Barbara was repatriated in a *lechero* plane that traveled to Mérida, Campeche, Veracruz, and finally to Laredo, where she was handed over to the North American authorities. The books the Beats wrote were prohibited in the Benjamin Franklin Library at the US Embassy in Mexico, which is decorated with a mural that contains a portrait of the "old beauty" Walt Whitman, as he was described by the poet Federico García Lorca.

44

A SONG

The shaman appeared at the doorway of her shack, barefoot, without a huipil, a walking stick, or a cigar. Under the sun that illuminated the mountainous landscape, she was resplendent.

María Sabina Magdalena García's silhouette faded bit by bit; she thinned; she became a shadow, a voice that sang out in an ecstatic rhythm:

Chjon Nka
Chjon Nca Catain
Jan Jesu Cri
Soso Soso
Santo
Santa
Santo
Kristros
Kristras
Kristros
Tsotsotsotsotsoooo
Ki so soso sooo

Sol
Solo
Sol
Sola
Tsotsotso
Santo
Santa
Santo
Santa

AUTHOR'S AFTERWORD

In Memory

Ever since the 1950s the name María Sabina has been intertwined with the ancient Mexican tradition of using hallucinogenic mushrooms. She is considered one of the last oral poets and one of the last surviving voices of ancient Mexico. Poets and anthropologists alike recognize her as the emblematic figurehead of an Indigenous culture that has used its voice to resist centuries of *mestizaje*, or racial mixing. Her songs, translated into Spanish, English, and other languages, and her role or character of shaman have come to represent the voice of the Mexican Indigenous woman. Her suffering and hardship in her later years are characteristic not only of the Mazatec but also other groups that practice rites of initiation to ecstasy, like the Tarahumara and the Huichol. If one were to see her, to hear her, one wouldn't consider the words of R. Gordon Wasson to be hyperbolic when he said of her: "Who knows? María Sabina could perhaps become one of the most famous Mexicans of her time. Long after other great figures of contemporary Mexico sink into oblivion, in the afterlife, her name and what she represented will remain engraved in the minds of men."

Of course, these words were spoken by a foreign mycologist, and not one historian of our own culture has accepted them as truth. She was an Indigenous poet who sang her songs in Mazatec and who was translated to English out of Spanish only after being translated from Mazatec into Spanish. Few of our own critics know of her, and few speak of her after her death. This is just one of the forms that our own cultural discrimination against the Indigenous world assumes. But R. Gordon Wasson was right: María Sabina was the foremost visionary poet of the twentieth century in the Americas.

Since 1955 (the year of the first velada recorded by R. Gordon Wasson), her litanies have had a great influence on the worlds of anthropology and literature. One day in February 1983, as my wife, Betty, and I were heading down Paseo de las Palmas in Mexico City, we read in a late edition of the newspaper that María Sabina was critically ill. It saddened us both greatly to hear this. That one of the greatest living poets of Mexico was dying in poverty was a tragedy. I remembered Wasson's words about her, and Betty and I decided to do whatever necessary to bring her to Mexico City to get her treatment. Meeting the venerable María Sabina was an opportunity to personally experience her great spirituality, but, more than that, the meeting affirmed the survival of the ancient Mexican world of magic, which has almost disappeared between the forces of social marginalization on one hand and the predatory nature of the government on the other. The very last time that I saw her, María Sabina looked like a creature so defenseless and so slight that her walking might have broken into flight.

May she rest in peace with her Holy Children, her illuminating mushrooms, those that she flew with and those with which she made others fly. Her songs of initiation into ecstasy: these were her birthright and are her legacy.

ACKNOWLEDGMENTS

Carne de Dios is a novel about the Beats' relationship to Mexico, and while in the narrative the focus of their pilgrimage is María Sabina and her mushroom ceremonies, in the larger history their journey was to the country itself. Mexico's history, landscape, and cultures were all fertile grounds for inspiration to the Beats, and the relationship between Mexico and this transnational communal countercultural and artistic movement is singular. The communal aspect of the Beat aesthetic is evidenced by the fact that they shared their burgeoning interest in and knowledge about Mexico at the time, just as they shared other shaping influences and inspirations. Homero Aridjis reflects this aspect of Beat culture in the novel by having his characters riff and elaborate on one another's words and ideas, some of which are faithfully quoted or paraphrased from previously existing texts. Adding to this is the fact that María Sabina, the center of this story, was an oral poet and a part of a larger oral tradition, so different source texts and recordings contain slight variations in transcriptions of her songs, which accounts for slight variations between her songs in the novel and her songs as printed elsewhere. Following this section is a list of source texts referenced both directly and indirectly in the novel, as well as further reading about María Sabina.

FURTHER READING ABOUT MARÍA SABINA

Archivo General de la Nación. 1956. "Investigación sobre conjura contra el Gobierno de la República de Cuba." Captain Fernando Gutiérrez Barrios, Federal Security Agency, Mexico City, June 24.

Benítez, Fernando. 1964. *Los hongos alucinantes*. Mexico City: Ediciones ERA.

Benzi, Mariano. 1972. *Les derniers adorateurs du peyotl*. Paris: Gallimard.

Bierhorst, John, trans. 1985. *Cantares Mexicanos = Songs of the Aztecs*. Stanford, Calif.: Stanford University Press.

Burroughs, William S. 1953. *Junky*. New York: Ace Books.

Burroughs, William S. 1981. *Cities of the Red Night*. New York: Rinehart and Winston.

Cowan, Florencia H. 1946. "Notas etnográficas sobre los Mazatecos de Oaxaca, México." *América Indígena* 6, no. 1 (January).

Cowan, George H. 1946. "Mazateco House Building." *Southwestern Journal of Anthropology* 2, no. 4.

Echevarría, Nicolás, dir. 1978. *María Sabina, mujer espíritu*. Mexico City: Centro de Producción de Cortometraje, Estudios Churubusco Azteca, RTC.

Estrada, Álvaro. 1977. *Vida de María Sabina, la sabia de los hongos*. Mexico City: Siglo XXI.

Ferlinghetti, Lawrence. 1955. *Pictures of the Gone World*. San Francisco: City Lights Books.

Ferlinghetti, Lawrence. 1958. *A Coney Island of the Mind*. New York: New Directions.

Frankl, Howard. 1963. "Me estoy volviendo loco." In *Antología de la poesía norteamericana*. Translated by José Coronel Urtecho and Ernesto Cardenal. Madrid: Aguilar.

García Lorca, Federico. 2002. *Collected Poems*. Edited by Christopher Maurer. Translated by Catherine Brown. Revised bilingual edition. New York: Farrar, Straus and Giroux.

Ginsberg, Allen. 1956. *Howl and Other Poems*. San Francisco: City Lights.

Ginsberg, Allen. 1961. *Kaddish and Other Poems, 1958–1960*. San Francisco: City Lights Books.

Góngora y Argote, Luis de. 2007. *Selected Poems of Luis de Góngora*. Translated by John Dent-Young. Bilingual edition. Chicago: University of Chicago Press.

Johnson, Jean Basset. 1939. "The Elements of Mazatec Witchcraft." *Ethnological Studies* no. 9. Switzerland: Gothenburg Ethnographic Museum.

Johnson, Jean Basset. 1939. "Some Notes on the Mazatec." *Revista Mexicana de Estudios Antropológicos* 3, no. 2. The anthropologist Johnson, who died in Tunisia during World War II at the age of twenty-nine, was the first "outsider" to attend a hallucinogenic mushroom ceremony, along with his team.

Kerouac, Jack. 1957. *On the Road*. New York: Viking Press.

Kerouac, Jack. 1958. *The Dharma Bums*. New York: Viking Press.

Kerouac, Jack. 1958. *The Subterraneans*. New York: Grove Press.

Kerouac, Jack. 1960. *Tristessa*. New York: Avon.

Lamantia, Philip. 1959. *Ekstasis*. San Francisco: Auerhahn Press.

Lamantia, Philip. 1967. *Selected Poems, 1943–1966*. San Francisco: City Lights Books.

Lamantia, Philip. 1981. *Becoming Visible*. Pocket Poets Series 39. San Francisco: City Lights Books.

Lamantia, Philip. 2013. *The Collected Poems of Philip Lamantia*. Edited by Garret Caples, Andrew Joron, and Nancy J. Peters. With a foreword by Lawrence Ferlinghetti. Berkeley: University of California Press.

Lowry, Malcolm. 1947. *Under the Volcano*. New York: Reynal & Hitchcock.

Lowry, Malcolm. 1962. "Delirium in Vera Cruz." In *Selected Poems of Malcolm Lowry*. Pocket Poets Series 17. San Francisco: City Lights Books.

Michaux, Henri. 2002. *Miserable Miracle*. Translated by Louise Var'ese and Anna Moschovakis. New York: New York Review of Books.

Morgan, Ted. 2012. *Literary Outlaw: The Life and Times of William S. Burroughs*. New York: W. W. Norton.

Motolinía [Toribio de Benavente]. 1971. *Memoriales o libro de las cosas de la Nueva España y de los naturales de ella*. Mexico City: Universidad Nacional Autónoma de México.

Münch, Vera Lawson. 1958. *Estaciones*. Bilingual edition with translations by Gerhart Münch and Armando Olivares. Guanajuato: Universidad de Guanajuato.

Munn, Henry. 1973. "The Mushrooms of Language." In *Hallucinogens and Shamanism*, edited by Michael J. Harner. Oxford: Oxford University Press.

Origen e historia de los reyes mixtecos: Libro explicativo del llamado Códice Vindobonensis: Codex Vindobonensis Mexicanus I. 1992. Introduction and explanation by Ferdinand Anders, Maarten Jansen, and Gabina Aurora Pérez Jiménez. Mexico City: Fondo de Cultura Económica.

Otto, Rudolph. 1923. *The Idea of the Holy.* Translated by John W. Harvey. Oxford: Oxford University Press.

Pound, Ezra. 1956. *Los Cantares de Pisa.* Translated by José Vázquez Amaral. Mexico City: Imprenta Universitaria.

Riedlinger, Thomas J. 1990. *The Sacred Mushroom Seeker: Essays for R. Gordon Wasson.* Portland, Ore.: Dioscorides Press.

Rimbaud, Arthur, Wallace Fowlie (trans.), and Seth Whidden. 2005. *Rimbaud: Complete Works, Selected Letters, a Bilingual Edition.* Chicago: University of Chicago Press.

Sabina, María. 1957. *Mushroom Ceremony of the Mazatec Indians of Mexico.* Recorded by V. P. and R. G. Wasson in Huautla de Jiménez, Oaxaca, Mexico, July 21, 1956. Smithsonian Folkways Records.

Sabina, María. 2003. *María Sabina: Selections.* Edited by Jerome Rothenberg. With texts and contributions by Álvaro Estrada and others. Berkeley: University of California Press.

Schultes, Richard Evans. 1939. *Plantae Mexicanae II: The Identification of Teonanácatl, a Narcotic Basidiomycete of the Aztecs.* Botanical Museum Leaflets, Harvard University, vol. 7, no. 3 (February): 37–54.

Schultes, Richard Evans, and Albert Hofmann. 1982. *Plantas de los dioses: Orígenes del uso de los alucinógenos.* Mexico City: Fondo de Cultura Económica.

Starr, Frederick. 1900–1902. "Notes upon the Ethnography of Southern Mexico." *Proceedings of the Davenport Academy of Sciences,* no. 9.

ViceVersa. 1998. Special issue, *Tras la huella de María Sabina.* No. 63 (August).

Villa Rojas, Alfonso. 1955. *Los Mazatecos y el problema indígena de la Cuenca del Papaloapan.* Mexico City: Memorias del Instituto Nacional Indigenista.

Wasson, R. Gordon. "Seeking the Magic Mushroom." *LIFE Magazine,* May 13, 1957, 100–120.

Wasson, R. Gordon. 1969. *Soma: Divine Mushroom of Immortality.* New York: Harcourt Brace & World.

Wasson, R. Gordon. 1974. *María Sabina and Her Mazatec Mushroom Veladas.* New York and London: Harcourt Brace Jovanovich.

Wasson, R. Gordon. 1980. *The Wondrous Mushroom: Micolatry in Mesoamerica.* New York: McGraw-Hill.

Wasson, R. Gordon. 1983. *El hongo maravilloso: Teonanácatl, micolatría en mesoamérica.* Mexico City: Fondo de Cultura Económica.

Wasson, R. Gordon, and Roger Heim. 1958. *Les champignons hallucinogènes du Mexique*. Paris: Editions du Muséum National d'Histoire Naturelle.

Watson, Steven. 1998. *The Birth of the Beat Generation: Visionaries, Rebels, and Hipsters, 1944–1960*. With an afterword by Robert Creeley. Circles of the Twentieth Century. New York: Pantheon Books.

Weitlaner, Robert J., and Irmgard Weitlaner. 1946. "The Mazatec Calendar." *American Antiquity* 11, no. 3 (January).

ABOUT THE AUTHOR AND TRANSLATOR

Homero Aridjis was born in Contepec, Michoacán, Mexico. He has written fifty-one books of poetry and prose and has won many important literary prizes, including the 2024 Griffin Poetry Prize. Formerly Mexico's ambassador to Switzerland, the Netherlands, and UNESCO, he is also the president emeritus of PEN International and the founder and president of the Group of 100, an environmentalist association of artists and scientists.

Chloe Garcia Roberts is a poet and a translator from the Spanish and Chinese. She is the author of a book of essays, *Fire Eater: A Translator's Theology*, and a book of poetry, *The Reveal*. Her translations include Li Shangyin's *Derangements of My Contemporaries: Miscellaneous Notes*, which was awarded a PEN/Heim Translation Fund Grant, and a volume of the collected poems of Li Shangyin, published in the New York Review Books / Poets series. She lives outside Boston and works as deputy editor of *Harvard Review* and as a lecturer of poetry at the Massachusetts Institute of Technology.

Library of Congress Cataloging-in-Publication Data
Names: Aridjis, Homero author | Roberts, Chloe Garcia translator
Title: Carne de dios : a novel / Homero Aridjis ; translated by Chloe Garcia Roberts.
Other titles: Carne de dios. English | Camino del sol
Description: [Tucson] : University of Arizona Press, 2025. | Series: Camino del sol : a Latinx literary series | Includes bibliographic references.
Identifiers: LCCN 2024049567 (print) | LCCN 2024049568 (ebook) | ISBN 9780816554140 paperback | ISBN 9780816554157 ebook
Subjects: LCSH: María Sabina, 1894–1985—Fiction | Lennon, John, 1940–1980—Fiction | Kerouac, Jack, 1922–1969—Fiction | Ginsberg, Allen, 1926–1997—Fiction | Burroughs, William S., 1914–1997—Fiction | Lamantia, Philip, 1927–2005—Fiction | Rulfo, Juan—Fiction | Castro, Fidel, 1926–2016—Fiction | Guevara, Che, 1928–1967—Fiction | Beats (Persons)—Fiction | Mushroom ceremony—Fiction | Huautla de Jiménez (Mexico)—Fiction | Mexico City (Mexico)—Fiction | San Francisco (Calif.)—Fiction | New York (N.Y.)—Fiction | LCGFT: Fiction | Novels | Biographical fiction
Classification: LCC PQ7297.A8365 C3713 2025 (print) | LCC PQ7297.A8365 (ebook) | DDC 863/.7—dc23/eng/20250331
LC record available at https://lccn.loc.gov/2024049567
LC ebook record available at https://lccn.loc.gov/2024049568